W9-DFG-760

GOLDEN WINDOWS
And Other Stories of Jerusalem

Also by Adèle Geras

My Grandmother's Stories:
A Collection of Jewish Folktales

Happy Endings

EGERTON HALL TRILOGY:
The Tower Room

Watching the Roses

Pictures of the Night

ADÈLE GERAS
GOLDEN WINDOWS

And Other Stories of Jerusalem

A Willa Perlman Book
An Imprint of HarperCollins*Publishers*

"Beyond the Cross-Stitch Mountains. 1948" was previously published in the United Kingdom by Hamish Hamilton under the title *Beyond the Cross Stitch Mountains* copyright © 1977 by Adèle Geras and illustrated by Mary Wilson.

~

Golden Windows
And Other Stories of Jerusalem
Copyright © 1993 by Adèle Geras
All rights reserved. No part of this book may be used or reproduced in any manner whatsoever without written permission except in the case of brief quotations embodied in critical articles and reviews. Printed in the United States of America. For information address HarperCollins Children's Books, a division of HarperCollins Publishers, 10 East 53rd Street, New York, NY 10022.
1 2 3 4 5 6 7 8 9 10
❖
First Edition

Library of Congress Cataloging-in-Publication Data
Geras, Adèle.
    Golden windows and other stories of Jerusalem / Adèle Geras.
        p.   cm.
    "Willa Perlman books."
    Contents: Golden Windows. 1910 — A garden with rabbits. 1912 — Beyond the Cross-Stitch Mountains. 1948 — Dreams of fire. 1950 — Cardboard boxes full of America. 1954.
    Summary: Five short stories that describe what it was like to grow up in Jerusalem in the first half of the twentieth century.
    ISBN 0-06-022941-1. — ISBN 0-06-022942-X (lib. bdg.)
    1. Children's stories, American. [1. Jews—Jerusalem—Fiction.
2. Jerusalem—Fiction.   3. Short stories.]   I. Title.
PZ7.G29354Go   1993   92-39885
[Fic]—dc20   CIP
                                                          AC

CONTENTS

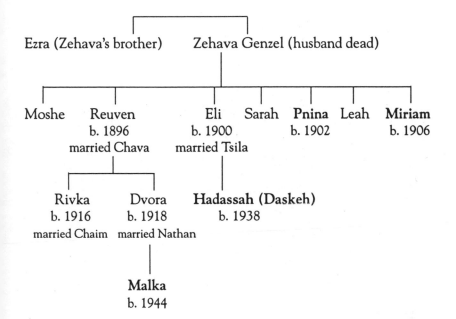

Ezra (Zehava's brother)   Zehava Genzel (husband dead)

Moshe	Reuven		Eli	Sarah	Pnina	Leah	Miriam
	b. 1896		b. 1900		b. 1902		b. 1906
	married Chava		married Tsila				

Rivka   Dvora   Hadassah (Daskeh)
b. 1916   b. 1918   b. 1938
married Chaim   married Nathan

Malka
b. 1944

GOLDEN WINDOWS
And Other Stories of Jerusalem

GOLDEN WINDOWS.
1910.

The Genzel family lived in four rooms on the second floor of a huge stone house that was arranged around the sides of a paved courtyard in one of the Jewish quarters of Jerusalem: the one called Me'a She'arim, The Hundred Gates. Eight households shared the building, but Zehava Genzel had more children than anyone else: Moshe, Reuven, Eli, Sarah, Pnina, Leah, and little Miriam. Pnina was eight years old.

"Poor Mrs. Genzel," the neighbors used to say. "So young and already a widow."

"But imagine if her husband had lived on!" whispered others. "There would be ten children in those rooms by now, and who knows how many more to come. Mr. Genzel, blessed be his memory, may have been taken up to heaven for a very good reason."

Pnina never thought of her family as especially large, nor did she mind the rooms where they all lived together being so crowded. She even quite enjoyed sharing a bed with Leah, especially during the winter. Leah was six, and slept so quietly that sometimes, in the morning, it looked as though she hadn't moved at all during the night. Once, Pnina decided to watch her through the dark hours, to see if she moved around in bed. For what seemed like a very long time, she stared at her sister lying motionless as a statue, but gradually Pnina's eyelids grew heavier and heavier and she fell asleep. In the morning, Leah's position in bed hadn't changed a bit.

Miriam, the youngest child, still slept in her crib next to her sisters' bed, and she used to snuffle and snort in her sleep like a little woodland creature burrowing among fallen leaves. The three boys shared the other bedroom, and Zehava and Sarah, her eldest daughter, slept in the living room, on beds that were covered up in the morning with bedspreads and cushions and turned into sofas for the rest of the day, until bedtime.

With so many in the family, Zehava Genzel made sure that every child helped her a little. Because she was the wanderer and loved to go walking in the streets and looking at everything, Pnina was the one chosen to fetch the bread from Greenberg's bakery. Usually, she took Leah with her, or even Miriam, because, as Zehava often said, "There's safety in numbers." Pnina couldn't see how Leah or Miriam would help her if she were in any great danger, and suspected that her mother was simply glad of the peace and quiet when the little children were out of the house.

One day in early December, though, Pnina went to get the bread by herself. Leah had a cough, and Miriam had fallen asleep on some cushions in a corner of the living room.

"It's a shame to wake her," Zehava whispered.

"I'll go by myself," Pnina whispered back, her heart making loud thumping noises in her ears for fear that her mother might not let her go. "I'll be very careful."

Zehava sighed. "Very well. I suppose not much harm can come to you between here and Greenberg's."

Pnina smiled. "So can I look in the windows as I go by, to see if I can find a present for Miriam's birthday?"

"I suppose so, but only on the main street. Don't turn off into any of the little alleyways."

"No," said Pnina. "I really won't."

She set out immediately. It had rained earlier in the day, but now a pale, chilly, wintery sort of sun hung in the blue sky. The pavestones were still wet, and the smell of damp pine needles filled the air. Pnina made her way down the hill, out of Me'a She'arim and into the part of the city that was full of shops selling silver and beaten copper and brass and carpets that vibrated with dark and glowing colors in spellbinding patterns. The streets were crowded with people shopping, and carriages drawn by mules, and beggars, and men selling delicious-smelling things to eat that her mother would never buy.

"You don't know how it's been cooked," she used to say. "It may be dirty and give you a terrible stomachache." Sometimes Pnina thought it would be worth having a stomachache, just to try a mouthful, but maybe not. Maybe a stomachache would never stop and she would be sick forever.

Pnina decided to buy the bread first and look for a present for Miriam on the way home. Mrs. Greenberg put the three braided loaves into the string bag for her, and said: "Such a big girl you're getting! Buying the bread all by yourself! For this you deserve a present."

"Thank you," Pnina said, and took a cinnamon-flavored cookie from Mrs. Greenberg's floury fingers. "I'll eat it while I'm walking."

Pnina never meant to break her promise to her mother. She had planned to go straight back along the main street, looking into all the familiar shop windows. She never knew exactly what it was that made her turn her head to the right, but something, some light, flashed at the very edge of her vision, and she looked down the tiny alleyway and saw the golden windows. Later, she realized that it must have been the sun, now a little lower in the sky, striking every pane of glass on that side of the street. But at the time it seemed to her as though a fiery apricot light were pouring out of every house, beckoning her, saying: Come. Come and look into all these golden windows and see what you will find.

She began to walk along the sidewalk. At first, she was disappointed. Close up, the panes of glass were no longer golden, and what shops there were, hidden among these tall, ancient-looking houses, turned out to be dusty and neglected. There was a cobbler's with a window full of broken shoes waiting to be mended, and a watchmaker's shop where one antique clock was on display, blanketed with beige dust.

"I should go home now," Pnina said to herself, and then she saw it. It was a window that seemed to have in it everything beautiful that was in the world. She could see sheets piled up in it, and embroidered pillowcases and tablecloths edged with ruffles of lace. There were petticoats and blouses hanging up and lying down. In one corner there was a heap of plump, satiny cushions and shawls and small rugs patterned with triangles and squares and wavy lines in scarlet, deep blue, purple, yellow and black. There was a piece of white velvet with rings and bracelets scattered all over it, and right at the front of the window, smiling out into the street, was a family of wooden dolls, each one smaller than the next, wearing head scarves and flowered aprons painted in colors so bright that they sang out to Pnina through the glass. As soon as she saw them, Pnina knew that she should buy them as a present for Miriam's birthday. Miriam would love them. She would go in and ask how much they cost. She opened the door and stepped into the dimness of the shop.

At first, Pnina thought that she had walked into the window by mistake. There were so many things pushed into the room, piled into the corners and hanging from all the walls, that she found it difficult to know exactly where to stand. At least there hadn't been any furniture in the window. Here, there were tables inlaid with mother-of-pearl, brass trays, marble ornaments, pottery vases, woven baskets, copper coffeepots, and on every flat surface more linen: crocheted bedspreads, sheets, pillowcases, and enough tablecloths for every table in Jerusalem. From the ceiling hung a variety of lamps and lanterns. Pnina looked around. There must be someone here whom she could ask about the dolls. She peered into the corners, and at last saw someone—a woman squashed into a small armchair.

"Excuse me," said Pnina, and the woman said: "How can I help you, little girl?"

As soon as she spoke, Pnina wanted to run away. This is not a real shop, she thought. The golden windows made me come here, drew me here. Hansel and Gretel were enchanted by all the candies and gingerbread that the witch's house was made of, and I've been made to come in here by those dolls. I've been made to come into a witch's shop. Pnina shivered. The old woman, who had left her chair and was coming closer and closer to her, was smiling, and because of her smile, because of her teeth, she had become the most terrifying person Pnina had ever seen. She had thin white hair pulled into a twist at the back of her head, and her pink scalp showed through the strands here and there. She was wrinkled. Her eyes were blue and watery. Her body was large and lumpy in places and covered in a black dress. But the teeth! Pnina knew she would have nightmares about them every night. They were broken and browny-yellow, and there were horrible gaps between them, and some were longer than others, and one even stuck out over the old lady's lower lip when she shut her mouth. In order not to see such a dreadful sight, Pnina looked down, and then she saw the hands that were nearly as hideous as the teeth: misshapen, twisted fingers covered with brownish blotches and speckles so that they looked like two old vegetables left behind on a market stall, or two tree roots hanging out of the long, black sleeves of her dress.

"I only wanted to know how much the dolls were. The family of dolls in the window."

"I will call my sister, Natalya," said the witch. "She is the one who deals with the prices. Natalya!" She opened her mouth wider to shout, so that Pnina could see more of her teeth. What would the witch's sister be like?

"I'm coming," said a voice from far away, and then a small door opened right at the back of the shop and a fat woman with a great deal of frizzy gray hair came to stand next to the witch.

"Natalya, dear, this child is asking the price of the dolls."

Natalya's eyes shone dark in a face like a ball of uncooked dough. Her fingers looked puffy and white, and over her gray dress she wore a flowered apron. At least her teeth are normal, thought Pnina. Suddenly she realized how late she was going to be.

"I have to hurry now," she said. "My mother is expecting me at home, but I would like to know the price of the dolls."

"Twenty-five piasters," said Natalya, and the witch nodded, as though she'd thought as much, all along.

"I'll bring the money next week," Pnina said, and she turned to go. As she reached the door, she called over her shoulder, "Thank you!"

The sisters were gazing after her. They seemed to be sorry she was leaving. Maybe they expected her to buy the dolls now. I wish I had the money, Pnina thought. Maybe they don't think I'll come back. They look so sad.

"I will come back," Pnina shouted. "I love those dolls so much."

She ran down the little alleyway toward the main road. The sun had moved on through the afternoon, and every window that had been brimming with gold was now a black square in the shadow of the buildings.

All the way home, Pnina thought about the dolls and how she wanted to keep them, and not give them to Miriam at all. Miriam, Pnina said to herself, will be four years old. She won't really care what she gets . . . but she'd love those dolls. Anyone would . . . but Miriam would perhaps love something else just as much. I could give her my pin in the shape of a heart . . . no, she might prick her fingers . . . well, there's the locket with space for a picture . . . but what would Mother say? She gave it to me last year. Pnina kicked the toes of her shoes along the sidewalk, grumpy because the only possible present for her sister was that beautiful set of dolls. She couldn't even buy the dolls and look around for something else for Miriam, because twenty piasters was all the money she had in the world, and although Zehava would give her five piasters toward Miriam's gift, she certainly wouldn't be able to afford more, and in any case, even if she were the richest woman in the world, money to buy a birthday present was meant for that purpose. You weren't supposed to spend all but a tiny bit of it on yourself. Pnina sighed. She was nearly at home. Soon it would be the Sabbath and candles would be lit and yellow light would fill every window in Jerusalem.

Pnina loved Friday evenings, with everyone freshly bathed and wearing their best clothes to greet the day of rest, and the smell of especially delicious food filling the house. She began to feel a little more cheerful. Perhaps, she thought, stepping into the courtyard of her building and glancing up toward the kitchen window, perhaps if Miriam has the dolls, it will be almost the same as having them myself. Maybe she will let me play with them. Climbing the stairs, she felt her heart heavy inside her like a small rock, and she knew it wouldn't be the same at all. Pnina wanted those dolls all to herself. She wanted to keep them on the shelf above her bed. She wanted no one else to touch them without her permission. She wanted to give them their names—special, magic names that only she, Pnina, would use. She knew that if she named them, they would come alive for her, they would become real people. If they were Miriam's, however often she was allowed to play with them, they would always be small wooden dolls, and nothing more.

"Wherever have you been, child?" Zehava cried, wiping her hands on her apron as she ran out of the kitchen. She'd been frying fish, Pnina knew, because her hands were still white from the flour and a sharp, golden-brown fragrance hung in the air.

"I'm sorry, Mother," Pnina said. "I would have come sooner, but I found such a shop! I've never seen such a shop. In the window there are so many things, you think the glass is going to break."

Zehava laughed. "It can only be the shop belonging to the Arlozoroff sisters! Did you see them? Olga and Natalya? They must be ancient now, poor creatures."

"Yes," said Pnina. "They are. The one called Olga looks like a witch. But they were very nice to me and they have a present that's just right for Miriam. I'm going to buy it next week."

"You can tell me all about it later. Now it's time

~

to get ready, and you're not even bathed yet. . . . Run, child, or the sun will set in the sky, and the Sabbath will be here before you've finished."

Pnina ran. As she waited for her mother to fill the tin bathtub with warm water, a thought came into her mind. She looked at her mother. "Why did you call them 'poor creatures'?" she asked. "If I had a shop filled with all those treasures, I'd think I was the luckiest person in the world."

"They're all alone," said Zehava. "Just the two of them, in that poky little room behind the shop. That's what I meant. Really, I should invite them one Friday evening. It's always a blessed thing to have guests to share your Friday meal."

"Then come with me next week, and I'll show you Miriam's present and you can invite them."

"Maybe," said Zehava. "We'll see what's happening next week. Maybe I'll come with you. Now will you kindly get into this water, and leave gossiping about the Arlozoroffs for another time?"

Pnina stepped into the bath. She was trying to calculate how long it would take her to save another twenty-five piasters—and then what if the dolls she had seen were the only ones? She tried to remember if there were any others in the shop at all. I can't remember seeing any, she thought, but in that crowded place they might have been hidden under something. Sitting as still as she could while Zehava scrubbed her back, Pnina thought: Only six more days and then I'll see them again, pouring their colors out of the golden window of that little shop. I wish the time would go quickly. I wish it would.

Pnina had never lived through such a slow week in her life before. The days stretched and stretched through more hours than seemed bearable, and the nights were filled with dreams, but at last Friday came and it was time for Pnina to buy the bread again.

"And will you come with me, Mother," she asked for the thousandth time that week, "and invite the Arlozoroffs? You promised."

Zehava laughed. "You forced me! You nagged me into it. Never have I seen such a persistent child. But you're right. I said I would invite them, so you can ask them if they'd like to come next week."

"Oh, no!" Pnina cried. "*I* can't ask them. You said *you* would. I'd never dare to ask them. I'd be frightened."

"Frightened of what, silly goose? They'll be delighted. Who asks them, after all, to go anywhere? You'll be doing them a favor."

"No," said Pnina. "I can't ask them. If you're not coming with me, then you must send a letter. A real invitation."

"Who's got time to write letters with four rooms to clean before lunch?"

"I'll get you the paper," said Pnina. "I know exactly where it is."

Zehava sat down at the table. "Very well," she said. "To put a stop to your ceaseless nagging, I will do anything. Bring me the paper, and also a pen and ink. Anyone would think I was inviting the Queen of Sheba and her sister!"

As she approached the shop, Pnina began to run. There was the alley, and yes, there at the top on the right-hand side, with the sun shining on it, turning it into a sheet of gold, was the window of the Arlozoroffs' shop. Pnina walked up to it and looked in, and suddenly the whole world turned dark. The dolls were gone. Pnina felt tears filling her eyes and spilling over to run down her cheeks. This was something she had never imagined, not even for one second. Someone else had come and bought them, the dolls that should have been hers, and couldn't be, but which at least would have been in her house where she could look at them. She very nearly turned and ran away, but then she remembered her mother's invitation and how she had promised to deliver it. She had to go into the shop.

Olga, the witchlike sister, was sitting in her armchair almost as though she hadn't moved at all since the previous week.

"Good day, child," she said. She stood up and began to walk toward Pnina. "Oh, it's you . . . the little girl who asked the price of the dolls."

Hearing the old lady mention them made Pnina hurt all over. She sank down onto a small wooden stool that happened to be positioned near the counter and started to howl and sob. The old lady put her hands to her head.

"Natalya! Natalya, come quickly! There's a child here crying. Natalya, what shall we do?"

Natalya bustled in from the back room.

"It's her," Olga said. "The child who wanted the dolls."

Natalya knelt down beside Pnina. "What's the matter, dear?" she said gently. "Have you perhaps lost your money?"

"Oh, no." Pnina sniffled and rummaged in her pocket to find the handkerchief in which her money was safely tied. "I've wrapped it up. Only now I need the handkerchief for my nose because I'm crying so much, and I don't need the money."

"Why not?" asked Natalya. "Have you changed your mind about the dolls?"

Pnina shook her head. "No," she said. "I haven't changed my mind . . . but they're gone! I've waited a whole week to buy them, and they're not here any longer. Some other child has them, and I'll never see them again."

"No, no," said Olga. "They're not in the window because we kept them for you. After you left last week, I said, 'We must put those aside for that child. If someone else buys them, she will be most upset.' They're in the back room. Come now, dry your eyes and have a short rest in our room to recover."

"Perhaps," said Natalya, "you will have a drink

while we wrap them up."

Pnina could feel her sadness disappearing as the sisters spoke. It was as though a thick woollen blanket of misery that had been covering her up were suddenly lifted off and thrown away. She flung her arms around Olga, who was standing right next to her.

"Oh, thank you! Thank you for keeping them! I love them so much! I'm so happy now. I feel as if I'll never cry again. Can we go and get them, please?"

"Certainly," said Natalya. "Follow me. Olga will wrap them up, and I will fetch you a drink and perhaps some sugared almonds."

The room at the back of the shop was the darkest place Pnina had ever seen. The tables and chairs were made of wood that looked almost black, and there was a black cupboard with carved doors towering in the corner. All over the walls were framed pictures of ladies in old-fashioned dresses and gentlemen in strange furry hats. There was one photograph of a baby in a lacy shawl.

"Is that your baby?" Pnina asked, pointing.

"No," Olga answered. "My youngest sister. Not

Natalya. The youngest one."

"Does she live here too?"

"She died," Olga said. "When she was about your age."

"Was she ill?" Pnina wanted to know.

"No . . . she was . . . we were all in a pogrom. A very terrible thing is a pogrom."

Pnina shivered. The strange word frightened her. "What is it?" she whispered.

"It is when bad people attack Jews . . . burn their houses, kill them as they are running away . . . even little children they kill. Natalya and I were the only ones left in our family, so we ran away to here. To Jerusalem." Seeing the frightened look on Pnina's face, the old woman smiled. "These are not good things for you to hear. Let us wrap the dolls and forget those horrors from days long ago." She opened a drawer in the sideboard and took out the largest of the dolls and set her on the table. Pnina stretched out a hand to touch the glossy paint on her head.

"She's so beautiful," she said, "but where are the others, the smaller ones?" A terrifying thought struck her. What if the dolls were twenty-five piasters each and she could only afford to buy one?

But Olga was smiling.

"You do not know? You have never seen dolls like this before? It's a special kind of doll called a Matrushka, and it comes from Russia." She took the doll in her hands and twisted it, as though she were wringing out a piece of washing. The doll split into two parts, and Pnina saw a smaller one inside. Olga took the second doll out, opened it to reveal the third one, and then the smallest doll appeared in her turn and smiled at all the others.

"Then," said Olga, "you put each one back together again like this . . . and you have four dolls. And when you are ready to pack them away, they go one inside the other again."

"Oh, that's wonderful," Pnina breathed. "It's the most wonderful surprise. I love them so much."

Natalya had come into the room and was pouring a red drink into tall glasses.

"You said they were for your sister's birthday," she said, and added: "Here, take a drink and a candy."

The sugared almonds lay like pale, prettily colored pebbles in a china dish. Pnina chose a mauve one, and said, "They *are* for Miriam's birthday. I wish they could be mine, but I can't afford two sets, and I can't even afford to buy them for myself and get another present for Miriam. I've thought and thought about it all week, and I've decided that if Miriam has them, then at least they will be in my house and maybe she'll let me play with them sometimes."

"You are a kind child," said Olga. "Take another sugared almond. Take a pink one. I always liked the pink ones best, because they are the color of pink blossoms. But now, of course, my days of eating sugared almonds are over. All my teeth would certainly fall out!" She cackled, looking more like a witch than ever, and Pnina was glad to be able to concentrate on the sweets and not have to gaze at that mouth.

"Oh," she said suddenly, "I nearly forgot. I have a letter for you both from my mother."

"A letter?" asked Natalya. "Do we know your mother?"

"My mother is Zehava Genzel," said Pnina, and at once both Olga and Natalya began to flutter and squawk around the table like a pair of ancient chickens. Natalya squawked loudest.

"Well, my goodness! Imagine—what a small

world! Zehava Genzel! Oh, her mother (your grandmother, blessed be her memory) was such a wonderful woman—and we knew your mother when she was your age. Olga, doesn't the child remind you of her grandmother, now that you know who she is?"

"Of course, of course! I knew she was a special child. How lovely! All these years . . . your mother used to like our shop when she was about your age. And now she is writing to us. Just imagine. What a happy day!"

The two women seemed content to pass the sealed envelope backward and forward over the table, smoothing it as though it were a beloved pet, admiring it as though it were a priceless jewel, and showing no curiosity at all about what it might say. Even though she knew what her mother had written, Pnina was growing more and more impatient. It was difficult to interrupt the flow of delighted chatter, but at last Olga and Natalya paused for breath, and she said quickly, "Don't you want to know what's *in* the letter? Aren't you going to read it?"

"I suppose so," said Olga. "But no one ever writes us a real letter . . . only bills of sale and business things . . . very boring . . . so this is a real treat for us. We are enjoying it."

"But the child has to go home, Olga," said Natalya. "Open it now and let us see what it says. We may have to send an answer with . . ." Natalya's hand flew to her mouth. "What a disgrace, little one! We haven't even asked your name. How rude we are!"

"It doesn't matter," Pnina said. "My name is Pnina."

"Lovely," said Olga. "Perfect! Pnina—a pearl. It suits you very well."

Pnina smiled, but she noticed that her mother's letter was still sealed. "Thank you," she said and looked pointedly at the envelope.

"We still haven't opened it," said Natalya. "I will fetch the letter opener."

By the time the letter opener was found in a drawer in the sideboard, by the time it had been polished with a corner of the tablecloth to remove every possible speck, by the time Olga had located her reading glasses behind a bowl filled with dusty-looking fruit, another ten minutes had passed. Then, at long last, Zehava's sheet of paper was unfolded, and Olga read the letter aloud.

"Well!" said Natalya, when she had heard it. "I'm quite overwhelmed. Such a kind invitation—how very exciting. Olga, we must answer at once. Where is the paper? The pen and ink?"

Pnina could imagine the minutes and minutes that writing an answer would take. She said, "Oh, no, please, my mother said you were not to worry about replying with a letter. I will take your answer back with me."

Olga nodded. "It is typical of such a fine person as your mother that she would spare us the least bit of trouble. How kind she is! How we are both longing to see her! Tell her we will be there next Friday at six o'clock and that we are most honored. Now we must wrap the dolls up and send you home, or your mother will wonder what has happened to you."

"And then," said Pnina, "they took ages and ages finding the right kind of tissue paper to wrap the dolls in. Everything took *so* long."

"Never mind," said Zehava. "We've given them a little pleasure in their lives. I will prepare a really nice meal for them, poor things."

"With nothing too hard to bite on," said Pnina.

"Olga's teeth are broken." She shuddered.

"Oh, nothing too hard." Zehava smiled. "I won't even put any nuts in the strudel. Now take those dolls and go and hide them away where Miriam won't see them. It was clever of you to find such a wonderful present. I'm surprised you don't want to keep them for yourself."

"I'll go and hide them," said Pnina. "Somewhere where they'll be safe till Tuesday."

Preparations for the Friday meal began early on Thursday morning.

"What a week!" said Zehava, as she ground up fish and chopped vegetables. "First Miriam's birthday and now this."

Pnina, Sarah and Leah were helping in the kitchen. The boys had been sent to get water and buy firewood. Little Miriam was sitting under the table with the set of dolls that Pnina had given her. They were her very favorite present.

"Will we be ready in time?" asked Sarah.

"Yes, of course," said Zehava. "I'm only making a few extra things."

But on Friday evening, it seemed to Pnina that the whole kitchen was bursting with gefilte fish, and mashed potatoes, and tureens of fragrant chicken soup, and different kinds of cakes, all without nuts so that Olga could eat them.

When the Arlozoroff sisters arrived, they were wearing their grandest clothes: leather gloves, and fur coats over their dresses, and lace collars fastened with amber pins and elegant hats pushed down to their eyebrows.

"Welcome!" said Zehava. "It is so many years since I've seen you, but you both look just the same."

"You are lying, of course," said Olga, "but we forgive you. How like your dear mother you look! And all these beautiful children! Pnina we know, of course, but all these others—how splendid! And this must be little Miriam, the birthday girl."

Miriam ran to hide in Zehava's skirts. Taking their coats off and settling down at the table seemed to Pnina to go on for a very long time. At last, though, the meal began. The dishes of food lay on the white tablecloth, the candlelight played on every face and threw shadows onto the wall, the wine sparkled in the best glasses.

"It is very many years," said Olga, "since we have had an evening as pleasant as this."

~

Pnina, who had been only half listening to the grown-ups talk about the old days, heard the remark and immediately thought of the shop. She thought of Olga and Natalya, hidden from everyone behind a high wall of linen and jewelry and furniture and ornaments, hidden in a small back room where dark cupboards loomed over them, and where the only people they ever saw were hanging on the wall in silver frames.

"When Pnina came into our little room," Olga was saying, just as though she had been reading Pnina's thoughts, "I think she was the first visitor we'd had since last year. Such a wonderful treat!"

"I will come to see you every week," said Pnina. "When I go to buy the bread."

"And me," Miriam piped up. "Pnina take Miriam!"

"Of course," said Natalya. "You should all come."

"But not all at once," said Olga. "There would not be room in the shop. We have too much stock!" She smiled. "It is because not many people buy from us, but we . . . we can't resist anything beautiful. We have to have it, so we buy it and put it in the window, which gets more and more full. One day the whole shop will explode and all our things will fly through the air and the whole of Jerusalem will be draped in our linen, and our jewelry will be scattered among the pavestones."

When the meal was over, Pnina stood up. "I have to put Leah and Miriam to bed now," she said to Olga and Natalya. "So I must say good night." As she spoke, she thought that perhaps her mother would tell her to kiss them both. She shivered. The teeth . . . well, she would close her eyes and hold her breath and kiss Olga's cheek very quickly and it would soon be over.

"But Pnina," said Natalya, "you must wait and open your present."

"It isn't my birthday till June," said Pnina.

"Nevertheless," said Olga, "we have brought presents. Sugared almonds for all the children, and some handkerchiefs for you, Zehava, and this small gift for Pnina." She burrowed in her handbag and handed the candies to Sarah and a small package to Zehava. For Pnina there was a small cardboard box.

"Thank you," said Pnina, thinking: Now I really *will* have to kiss them. Whatever can this be?

Inside, the box was filled with tissue paper—but there was something hard . . . something rounded . . . a doll . . . a doll like Miriam's! Pnina pulled the tissue away.

"Oh! Oh! I can't believe it. Are they really for me? Really? They're beautiful. So beautiful—even lovelier than Miriam's. Oh, I love you!" Pnina ran to Olga and Natalya and kissed and hugged them, one after the other. "This is the best present I've ever had."

Pnina opened the biggest doll and took the others out and lined them up on the table for everyone to admire.

"This one I shall call Olga, after you," she said, "and the next one Natalya."

The two old ladies smiled.

"Now," said Pnina, "I need two more Russian names."

"Our mother was Sonya," said Olga. "That's a pretty name."

"And the littlest one can be Tamara," said Natalya. Pnina knew as soon as Natalya had spoken that Tamara was the name of the baby in the photograph, the one in the lacy dress, the one who had been killed long ago in a pog-something.

Pnina had forgotten the word, but she remembered the baby's face. She looked at the two old ladies, both suddenly very quiet, and saw that their eyes glittered in the light of the candles as though they were filled with tears.

Pnina found it hard to fall asleep that night. The dolls—Olga, Natalya, Sonya and little Tamara—were lined up in the dark. In the moonlight she could see the shapes they made against the wall. Leah was asleep, and not moving. Miriam was snuffling and snorting in her crib. Pnina got out of bed and went to the window. She wasn't the only person in the city who was awake so late. Here and there, there were places where a candle still flickered, there were still some golden windows in the darkness of the night.

A GARDEN WITH
RABBITS.
1912.

"Why does it always have to be me?" Pnina said. "Why can't anyone else take Miriam out for her walk?"

"You know very well," said Zehava, "that everyone else is busy. The boys have gone to help Uncle Ezra in the shop, Sarah is making oznei Haman with me for Purim, and Leah has gone to spend the day with Rachel."

"I could make oznei Haman instead of Sarah,"

Pnina suggested. Oznei Haman were the triangular cakes shaped like ears filled with honey and poppy seeds that everybody ate at Purim, when they dressed up in fancy costumes, and remembered the story of brave Queen Esther and the wicked Haman, who died in the end as a punishment for his evildoing.

"Eating the cakes you are good at and you enjoy," Zehava laughed. "But making them has always bored you. That's what you say when I call you to help me in the kitchen. Picking up a dishcloth and drying a fork is for you a big achievement. I should have thought you'd much rather walk around Jerusalem, especially on such a beautiful day."

"I don't mind walking," said Pnina, and it was true. Of all the Genzel children, Pnina knew the city best: the wide roads winding down the hill, the buildings made of yellow stones that glittered in the sun, and the narrow streets where tall houses with shuttered windows cast deep, cool shadows even when the sun was at its fiercest.

"Then what *do* you mind?" her mother asked.

"Having to listen to Miriam's questions every single minute. Do you know, she can hardly manage to breathe properly, she talks so much. She wants to know everything. It's exhausting. Also, she never wants to come where I want to take her. She wants to look at the shops, or else go down past the hospital, or else up to the market."

"And where would you like to go?"

"I like all the little streets. I like the quiet places where not many people go. I like looking at all the windows and imagining who lives there. Miriam says that's boring."

Zehava said, "As a special favor to you, then, I will tell Miriam that you are both to go wherever *you* decide, and if she complains, you are to bring her straight home. Will that do?"

"I suppose so," said Pnina. "I'll go and get ready. If we're going, we may as well start. Will you save a bit of the poppy seed mixture for me to taste when I come home?"

"Can't you wait till Purim comes?"

"No," said Pnina. "I want a taste today. I'm sure that's the only reason Sarah has agreed to help you—so she can have little tastes of everything as she works."

Zehava laughed. "Those little tastes are a cook's reward for making lovely food for everyone, but I notice it's never been enough to tempt you into the kitchen."

"But today you will save me a little, won't you? As a reward for listening to Miriam all afternoon?"

"Just a teaspoonful," said Zehava, "and you'd better go soon, or the day will have become night. I'll find Miriam now and get her ready."

"And tell her she has to obey me completely— go exactly where I want her to go for a change."

"I will bribe her with a teaspoonful of poppy seed and honey. She is almost as greedy as you are."

"Can we go this way now?" Miriam asked. "Please, Pnina, we've been walking along your streets for hours and hours and there hasn't been a single shop. I've only seen six people all afternoon, and three of them have been very old men who don't count at all."

"So who *does* count?" Pnina thought she'd never heard such nonsense in her life. Whatever went on in her little sister's head?

"Ladies count," said Miriam, "especially if they have hats on, and handsome young men and babies. They're the best. Can we go this way now? There's a shop that sells jewels down there, I know there is. We went past it once with Mother on our way to Eva the dressmaker's, but she wouldn't stop."

"You're thinking of some other street," said Pnina. "This is nowhere near where Eva lives."

"It is! I'm sure it is! Let's at least go and have a look."

"No," said Pnina. "I don't want to go down there. I want to go this way."

"Well, I don't."

"It doesn't matter what you want. Mother said you had to obey me."

"I've obeyed you for hours."

"You have to keep obeying me till we get home."

"Then," said Miriam, "I want to go home now and stop obeying. I don't like it."

"I don't care," said Pnina. "Because I say we're not going home yet. I want to go down this street."

"I'm going to sulk," Miriam announced, pulling her pretty round face into what she hoped was a dreadful, fierce scowl. "I'm going to sulk till we get home. I won't say a single word to you. I'll stop talking to you. That'll be your punishment."

"How lovely!" said Pnina. "My ears could do with the rest. Chatter, chatter, chatter, that's all you do all day long. A little silence will come as a pleasant relief." Miriam snorted, but she followed her sister.

She won't be able to keep up this silence till we get home, Pnina thought. Especially if I keep talking to her. In the end she'll just have to answer, or she'll burst. And I'm going to go on talking, oh yes! I'm not having her telling Mother I didn't say a word. I'll be completely normal and friendly. Miriam won't have a thing to complain about. I'll tell stories about the people in these houses to make her laugh. Pnina looked at her sister, whose nose was pointed toward the sky in a way that said very clearly, "Do whatever you like. It's no business of mine."

"Miriam," she said. "Bring your nose down from up there and enjoy this street. There are some very exciting people living here." The nose remained fixed on the heavens. "Not everyone knows this, because it looks like an ordinary street, but it isn't. It isn't at all. It's a very special street. Should I tell you who lives in this house, for instance?"

The upturned nose gave a haughty sniff. Well, thought Pnina, I know she's listening. Probably she's bursting to ask me all kinds of questions. Let me think of some really fantastical tales. . . .

"In that house, there lives a woman who turns into a bear every evening. Truly. She can't help it. Her children have to make sure she never goes out at night. They never tell anyone, and try to keep her indoors after dark, of course, but once she left the house in the evening and I happened to see her. She won't hurt us now. It's daylight and she looks quite normal. In fact, she wouldn't even hurt us at night. She's a very friendly sort of bear and her family is all devoted to her, but still, I don't think I'd like to see her again. The very worst thing of all was those big, hairy paws in lacy gloves—ugh!" Pnina gave an elaborate shudder. She glanced at Miriam, whose nose was definitely lower by a couple of inches. What was more, she wasn't slouching and dragging along the sidewalk: she was walking quite briskly. She doesn't want to miss a word of what I'm saying, Pnina thought. I'd better not stop.

"Here," she said, "there lives a man whose arms and legs are made of wood. He looks all right from the outside, so that you could never tell, but he was very badly hurt one day when he fell off his horse, and they had to give him specially carved wooden arms and legs. He walks a little stiffly, naturally, and wears his sleeves extra long to hide his arms and most of his hands, but otherwise he's just like anyone else. There's a special hospital he went to in Vienna where they make wooden limbs. They're all hanging in this huge room, rows and rows of arms and legs in all shapes and sizes, and if you are hurt, all you have to do is go to the hospital and choose—it's almost as easy as buying shoes or gloves."

As she spoke, Pnina was so carried away by the story of the man with wooden arms and legs that she walked along without really paying attention to where she was. In the maze of tiny, twisted streets that lay behind the huge magnificence of the Russian Orthodox church, she turned first along a road that went to the left, then down another tempting street with Miriam following behind her, listening, until at last the girls found themselves on a long, sloping road where a cool silence lay over the stones and there was no visible sign of people. The girls walked and walked, and at last Pnina finished the story and turned to see how her sister was enjoying it, but Miriam was no longer keeping up with her. She was about fifty yards away, standing at a tall gate made of iron curled into elaborate patterns, which Pnina had vaguely noticed out of the corner of her eye as she passed it.

"Miriam!" Pnina called. "Come here this minute! What are you doing? It's rude to look so hard into people's gates like that." As she spoke, Pnina retraced her steps to where her little sister stood on tiptoe, with her head almost through the metal railings. Miriam turned as she approached. All the scowls had disappeared and instead she looked like a picture of the sun drawn by a child—happy and bright and with a smile so wide, it stretched from one side of her face to the other.

"Pnina, look!" she said. "Look what I've found!"

"Ah! So we've finished sulking then, have we?"

"Sulking's stupid," said Miriam. "This is so lovely. Come and see. Oh, you're clever, Pnina.

You knew this garden was here all the time, didn't you? You wanted it to be a surprise. Thank you."

Pnina came to stand beside her sister. She, too, peered between the metal railings. She saw a quiet courtyard, with a small fountain in the center surrounded by white flagstones. All around the fountain there were enormous pottery urns filled with new flowers, just opening for the spring, and in one corner, a tree with white blossoms rose almost as high as the balcony. There were other trees in the courtyard as well—small palms and pepper trees and little cypress trees, also in pots. There were cacti growing in one corner, and in another . . .

"Pnina," said Miriam, "look over there. Can you see? There are rabbits."

"Oh, yes," said Pnina. "I can see them. I can see a black-and-white one and a white one. Oh, they're so beautiful!"

"Let's go in," Miriam said. "Let's go in there and look at them."

"We can't," Pnina said. "This is someone's house. We can't possibly just march in there and pet the rabbits."

"Why not?"

"We can't, that's all."

"But we won't hurt them," Miriam begged. "Please, Pnina, just for a moment. We'll just touch them for a minute and then go—and look how quiet it is. Maybe everyone has gone out."

Pnina sighed. "I suppose there isn't any harm." She, too, wanted a closer look at the rabbits, and Miriam was hopping up and down with excitement.

"Come on, then, just for a second." Pnina noticed a keyhole and looked at it carefully. Then she tried to push down the latch on the metal gate, but it refused to move.

"The gate is locked, Miriam. We can't go in. I'm so sorry."

Miriam sighed. "Will you bring me again tomorrow?"

"Yes," said Pnina. "I'll bring you again, but now I think we should go home."

"Yes," said Miriam.

Pnina wasn't quite sure of the way home, but she had no intention of telling her younger sister. I will find it, she thought. If I turn left here, and start walking uphill, then eventually I will come to somewhere I recognize. The girls walked and walked, and at last they arrived at the florist's shop just down the road from where they lived. Pnina felt safe again. She turned to her sister.

"You haven't been speaking much," she said. "I thought sulking was over."

"I haven't been sulking," Miriam answered. "I've been thinking about those rabbits."

"Yes," Pnina said. "So have I."

This wasn't entirely true. Pnina had been worrying. First she had worried about finding the way home, and now that they were nearly there, another, even greater worry filled all her thoughts. She had promised to take Miriam back to visit the rabbits next day, and she didn't think she could remember how to reach the house. Down to the Russian Orthodox church, and then was it left or right? And whatever would Miriam say if she could never find them again? Pnina went on worrying about this on and off for the rest of the day and far into the night. After everyone else had gone to sleep Pnina lay awake trying to retrace in her mind the path she had taken earlier in the day.

"What do you mean, you don't know where they

are?" Miriam's brow was darkening, her mouth beginning to turn down at the corners. "You promised me yesterday to bring me back to see the rabbits. Why didn't you say *then* that you wouldn't be able to find them?"

"Well . . ." Pnina searched around desperately for an excuse. "Yesterday I thought I *would* be able to find them, but now I can't."

"Can't we look for them a bit longer?" Miriam asked, her voice wobbling dangerously.

"No!" said Pnina. "We have to go home now."

"I don't *want* to go home," Miriam shouted. "I want to find those rabbits. You said we could."

"I want to find them too," Pnina shouted back. "Just as much as you do. There's no need to get angry about it. That doesn't help anyone."

"I don't care! I don't care! I want to see them," Miriam shrieked. Pnina sighed, and looked around anxiously. Thank goodness there's no one in the street, she thought. I must get her home quickly. Miriam's tantrums were famous in the building where the Genzels lived. They broke over the house like thunderstorms: noisy, dark, wet and frightening; but like storms, they didn't last long, and her brothers and sisters had long ago learned that the best way to get through them was simply to wait until they had worn themselves out. That's all very well at home, thought Pnina, as she took her little sister's hand and began to drag her through the streets. Out here in the open, if anyone sees me, goodness knows what they'll think. Maybe they'll think I've been hitting her. Maybe I *should* hit her. Perhaps it'll stop her wailing. Pnina pulled Miriam behind her, quickened her steps and nearly broke into a run in her anxiety to reach the safety of her own house. She turned into a road that sloped upward and looked around her. Was this, could this possibly be, the right way? She sighed. She was so eager to get Miriam away from prying eyes that she had almost forgotten to notice where they were. The street was empty, but, Pnina thought, that didn't mean that people weren't staring out their windows, using the edges of their curtains to hide behind. Miriam's howls were quieter now. She was out of breath from keeping up with her sister, because it is difficult to howl and run at the same time. Instead of howling, Miriam had turned to sniffing and loud sighing. Then, suddenly, Pnina stopped.

"Miriam," she whispered. "I think I've found the house. Isn't this it? Look, there's the gate."

"Oh!" Miriam was too overcome to speak. She gasped and looked through the railings. Yes, there were the black-and-white rabbit and his white brother, both pressing their noses against the wire netting of their hutch.

"They want to see us," said Miriam. "Look! The white one is standing on its back paws and waving its ears at us." She jumped up and down and called out, "Wait, little rabbits! We're coming! We're coming!"

"Shh!" said Pnina. "Do you have to announce it to the world? We're not supposed to be here, going into strange gardens, and anyway, the gate could still be locked, do you remember? I *did* tell you the gate could be locked, didn't I?"

"Yes," said Miriam. Pnina looked a little less worried. At least there wouldn't be another tantrum-tempest if they couldn't get in. "But you must at least try."

"Very well," said Pnina. She tried the gate and it was open. It wasn't until that very second that she realized how much she had been hoping that it would be closed. Miriam began squeaking loudly.

"Be quiet!" Pnina hissed. "You sound like a crazy mouse. And you'll have the whole household coming to see what the noise is if you're not careful." She looked around the silent courtyard. Nothing stirred. Even the rabbits were quite motionless, apart from their little twitching noses.

"Come on," Pnina whispered, and she stepped into the courtyard with Miriam following closely behind her. The girls tiptoed across the white flagstones, past the terra-cotta urns brimming with flowers under the scented fronds of the pepper tree, and over to the corner where the wooden hutch stood. As the girls came closer, the rabbits became quite excited.

"Maybe they think we're bringing them food," said Pnina.

"We should have brought them some scraps from home," said Miriam. "Now they won't like us."

"Of course they'll like us," said Pnina. "They look very fat to me. I'm sure whoever owns them looks after them very well."

"Next time," said Miriam, "I will bring them some pieces of carrot."

"Shh," said Pnina. "Don't talk." She wanted to change the subject. She had no intention of coming here again, but she didn't know how to tell Miriam. Perhaps she would ask their mother to forbid it; then Miriam's storms of tears would have to be dealt with by someone else. She looked at her sister. Miriam had pushed her chubby forefinger through the wire netting and was stroking the black-and-white rabbit's nose. The white one seemed a little shy, a little unwilling to come forward and claim attention.

"Snowy," Miriam whispered, trying to entice him. Snowy! Pnina thought. What a boring name for a white rabbit. Surely they could think of something better? Blossom? Star? Fluffy? She was pondering names when the voice boomed out from behind her.

"What are you girls doing, may I ask?" it said, and both Pnina and Miriam whirled around, terrified. The owner of the booming voice was enormous: a huge man with a long, black beard and a long black jacket. He was limping across the courtyard toward them, leaning on a walking stick. For one horrible moment, Pnina thought that her story about the man with wooden arms and legs had come true, but no, she could see, now that the man was very close to them, that his hands, anyway, were real. Real and hairy, covered with a kind of dark fur, almost to his fingernails. She shuddered and felt Miriam taking her hand and drawing closer. Perhaps this was a person who sometimes turned into a wolf. She spoke, and her words sounded like the chirpings of a frightened bird.

"Please, sir, we're sorry. We are really doing no harm. My sister and I . . . we saw the rabbits yesterday, and since we were passing the house today we thought that just one tiny pet wouldn't hurt anyone. My sister is so fond of animals."

"Well," said the man. "No harm has been done, I suppose, but if I'd wanted children coming in from the streets to stroke the rabbits that belong to my son, then I would have had a sign hung outside saying Zoological Gardens." He thought that this remark was very amusing and smiled, showing big, square, pale-yellow teeth.

Pnina said again, "We're sorry. We won't come back, I promise," and she began to edge away slowly toward the gate.

"Then I will say no more about it," said the huge hairy man. "Come, I will make sure to lock the gate after you."

The turning of the key in the lock echoed in the stillness of the afternoon. Pnina and Miriam stood outside the gate, watching the man limp back toward the house, his stick tapping on the stones of the courtyard.

"He's gone," said Miriam. "I'm glad. He was really horrible. Wave good-bye to Snowy and Spotty."

Spotty! That was even worse than Snowy. Surely they could find better names? Pnina was on the point of opening her mouth to say so, when she suddenly realized that they would never be seeing the rabbits again. At least she hadn't been the one to break the bad news.

"Can we come back tomorrow?" Miriam said, and Pnina sighed.

"No, Miriam. Didn't you understand what that man was saying? He said we mustn't come back. He said the rabbits belong to his son."

Miriam smiled. "He said that we mustn't go in. He didn't say we couldn't look from the gate."

"But where's the fun in looking?" Pnina cried. "We won't be able to touch the rabbits, and you'll feel really upset in the end. I know you will."

"Not 'the rabbits,'" said Miriam. "Snowy and Spotty."

"Why did you choose those names?" Pnina asked.

"Because," said Miriam, smiling radiantly, "I think they're lovely. Don't you think they're lovely names?"

Well, what difference does it make after all? Pnina thought. They're not our rabbits. "Lovely names," she said. "It was clever of you to think of them."

Miriam skipped along the pavement, all the way home.

The next day, Miriam was ill. She felt, she said, "wobbly and sore and hot" at lunchtime, and Zehava put her to bed. All the children took turns sitting with her, and holding cool wet cloths over her forehead, and tried to persuade her to drink the milk, soup and juices that Zehava prepared. Sometimes she tried a few drops, and from time to time she fell asleep, but when she was awake, she tossed and turned in her small bed. Her dark curls lay damp on her cheeks, and her eyes were too bright. The doctor came and prescribed some green medicine, but Miriam refused to take it.

Then next day when it was Pnina's turn to sit with her, she told Miriam long stories about the adventures of Snowy and Spotty. The rabbits went to the seaside near Jaffa, they dressed up for Purim, they took a ride in a horse-drawn carriage to the hills outside the city. Pnina was trying so hard to think of new adventures that after a while her head was in a whirl. Then she noticed that two fat tears were sliding out of the corners of Miriam's eyes.

"What are you crying for?" Pnina asked. "Don't you like my stories?"

"Yes, I like them, but they make me sad."

"They're supposed to make you happy." Pnina sighed. "I'll stop if you don't like them."

"I *do* like them, but I want to see the real rabbits. I want to stroke Snowy and Spotty. I really, really do."

Pnina had a sudden brilliant idea. "Will you drink your medicine and all your soup and drinks and try very hard to get better if I promise you that you can pet the rabbits?"

Miriam sat up in bed. "Oh, yes, Pnina! I'll drink the whole bottle of medicine all at once."

"Mother!" Pnina shouted, and Zehava came running in from the kitchen, wiping her hands on her apron. "Mother, Miriam has promised me to drink all her drinks and take all her medicine and get better as quickly as she possibly can."

"Thank God!" cried Zehava, and Pnina realized how many days it was since her mother had looked really happy. There were dark shadows under her mother's eyes. Pnina knew that Zehava had sat next to Miriam's bed all through the night. It was no wonder she was tired.

"I'll go and get some chicken soup this very minute," Zehava said. "And the medicine."

When she had left the room, Miriam asked, "How will you manage it, Pnina? That hairy man told us not to come back."

"Leave it to me," said Pnina. "I have an amazing secret plan."

The next afternoon, Pnina walked alone through the maze of streets behind the Russian Orthodox church. She knew the way a little better now. It's down here, she said to herself, and then right by that house with green shutters. I must make sure not to step on any cracks in the pavement. If I can do that, it'll be all right. Miriam will get better quickly, and we'll be allowed to visit the rabbits. She wished that what she had told Miriam about an amazing secret plan were really true. Without such a plan, Pnina didn't know what would happen when she reached the house. Or rather, she thought that she did know, and was very nervous indeed. She would have to ring the bell, ask to see the hairy man and tell him the whole story. Perhaps he only *looks* horrible and has a very kind heart, said Pnina to herself. But he threw us out the other day, so how kind can he be? She shook her head miserably. I'll just have to try my hardest. I'll tell him my sister got sick from wanting to visit the rabbits. Maybe there's even some truth in that. She tiptoed over one crack, then another. Nearly there.

When she arrived at the house and looked between the railings, the hairy man was nowhere to be seen. Instead, a skinny boy with a long neck and sandy hair was standing next to the hutch.

He had his back to her. Pnina thought: This must be the hairy monster's son. He doesn't look a bit frightening. What a miracle! And the rabbits actually belong to him. If he gives permission for them to be petted, then what can anyone do to stop it?

"Hey!" Pnina called out. "Excuse me! Hey! Could you please come over here a minute?" The boy whirled around to face her. He looked terrified. Pnina was intrigued. Why would this boy, who was about Eli's age, be frightened of a younger girl?

"M-m-me?" he said, so quietly that Pnina could hardly hear him.

"Yes, you," said Pnina. "I'd like to talk to you, but it's difficult when you're standing way over there. Can you come here, please, to the gate?"

The boy made his way across the courtyard so slowly that Pnina nearly shouted out "I won't bite you" but then decided against it. She knew from observing her brothers that boys didn't like admitting they were scared. Instead, as he drew closer, she called out what she thought of as a friendly remark: "Hello, what's your name?"

He was right beside the railings now. Pnina could have easily reached through the bars of the gate to touch him.

"D-D-David," he said, and blushed crimson and looked at his feet.

"I'm Pnina," she said, and realized why the poor boy had been so nervous about speaking to her. He had a bad stammer and clearly found it very hard to make conversation with people. Pnina wondered whether it would be rude to mention his stammer or whether she should pretend not to notice it. In the end she decided to speak her mind.

"Hello, David," she said. "It's a pleasure to meet you. I hope you don't mind speaking to me. I know it's a bit hard for you to answer, but I really don't mind waiting to hear what you say, so don't feel bad about it and blush every time you open your mouth." She smiled, and to her surprise, David smiled back.

"W-w-w-why did you come b-b-ack?" he said. "I s-s-aw you and your s-s-sister. M-m-my father d-d-doesn't want me to b-b-be embarrassed, so he d-d-doesn't l-l-let many p-p-p-people come here. I h-h-haven't g-got many friends." David seemed out of breath at the end of such a long sentence.

"We'll be your friends, and we'd love to come and visit you," Pnina said quickly. "My little sister's sick, and she likes your rabbits so much that I promised her to come and ask your father for permission to pet them sometimes."

"They're m-m-m-my rabbits," David said. "I g-g-give you permission. Will you t-t-t-talk to me when you c-c-come?"

"Yes, of course," said Pnina. "But shouldn't you ask your father?"

"Ask your father what?" said the booming voice. The hairy man had crept up on them.

Pnina trembled a little, but she said as bravely as she could, "Good afternoon! I've come to ask permission to visit the rabbits. My sister wants to so much that she's got a fever from so much wanting!"

"Good heavens!" said the hairy monster. "What have you said to this young lady, David?"

"I've said they c-c-could c-c-come and p-p-p-play with the rabbits."

"Well," said the hairy monster, "I suppose there's no reason why they shouldn't."

"We can talk to David as well," said Pnina,

"and David can come to our house and be our friend. I have a brother called Eli who would like a new friend, I know. Maybe David could come home with me now."

The hairy monster said, "Just to accompany you then, as it's getting a little late—but be sure to come straight back, David."

"My mother will never let him go home without giving him food," Pnina said. "Nobody comes into our house and leaves without eating."

"That's very kind of you," said the hairy monster. "I will look forward to seeing you and your sister again when you come to visit the rabbits."

"Thank you, sir. My sister will be so happy."

David and Pnina walked in a friendly sort of silence for most of the way to the Genzels' house. Then Pnina said, "That's where I live—come on!"

David hesitated. "I d-d-don't know if I sh-sh-should," he began.

"That's silly!" said Pnina, taking hold of his hand as though he were Miriam. "Everyone will be so pleased to meet you. For my little sister you're already a hero, because you're the owner of Snowy and Spotty."

David laughed. "S-s-snowy and Sp-sp-spotty!" he exclaimed. "What funny names! Their real names are Benny and Boaz."

"Don't tell Miriam," said Pnina. "She thinks Snowy and Spotty are wonderful names. Come and meet my brothers. Come and meet Eli."

David climbed the stairs behind Pnina. She burst into the house, shouting, "Miriam! Miriam! Look who's here! It's David, the owner of the rabbits." Then she ran into the bedroom to tell her sister the whole story. Zehava came to see what all the noise was all about.

"Hello," she said to David. "How nice to see you. Come and sit down and eat a piece of apple cake. Eli, come and meet this new friend."

Eli came to the table. "I'm Eli," he said smiling. "What's your name?"

"D-D-D-David."

"Well, hurry up and finish your cake, and I'll show you my special climbing tree."

David smiled and began to eat.

"Leave the poor boy alone," said Zehava. "Let

him eat without choking. There'll be plenty of time for trees." Pnina came into the room.

"David," she said, "Miriam's better. She's really better. And she wants to meet the boy who owns the rabbits."

"Will you go and tell her to wait?" said Zehava. "The poor child can't even finish a bit of cake in peace. Tell her he's coming in a minute."

"And after that," said Eli, "after you visit Madame Miriam, then I'll show you my tree."

David nodded happily and took another bite of cake.

BEYOND THE CROSS-STITCH
MOUNTAINS.
1948.

*H*adassah (always called Daskeh) was wiping the clean counter even cleaner with her damp cloth. Soon, the grocery shop, hollowed into the wall of yellow stone like a small, dark cave, would close for the Sabbath. Daskeh's father, Eli Genzel, was in the back room, sitting at a small table and poking with a spoon at the slice of lemon in his tea.

"This lemon will have to go," he muttered.

"How many cups can the poor thing float in without falling to bits? No flesh left, only brown rind."

Daskeh answered from the shop. "And you're lucky to have that, as you always say to me." She put the cloth away and came to sit with her father at the table.

"Are you ready to close, child?" he said.

"Close, open, what's the difference? There's so little to sell, these days. Except smells. I can't scrub them out. Pickled herring, brown bread, soap—all the smells hanging around the shop like ghosts. They won't go away."

"They are to remind us of happier days, maybe . . ."

"Maybe. But they make me feel sad. The cheese went this morning. Five hundred grams. I must have cut slices for the whole street. I'll be the best slicer of cheese in the whole of Jerusalem soon. Transparent bits of cheese, I make. Nothing in them, hardly." Daskeh poured some pale liquid from the teapot into a glass.

Eli ran his thumb along the wrinkles in his brow and said, "Transparent cheese is cheese. No cheese is no cheese."

"Transparent cheese is just as bad as no cheese,

when you refuse to take money for it."

"We must share, these days. And besides, there is so little to buy, what do we need money for?"

Daskeh was silent. She was drinking her tea and thinking of sugar. She thought about putting four cubes into her glass, remembering the way they lost their shape and crumbled into the liquid and were whirled around by her spoon like tiny grains of diamond. She said, "When this is all over, I'll put six cubes of sugar into every cup of tea."

"Then it will be too sweet." Eli smiled.

"Then I'll pour it down the sink, and make another cup. As many cups as I like. As strong as I like. All day long."

"Isn't it time you went home to help your aunt prepare the Sabbath meal, such as it is? Go, child—I'll close up the shop."

Daskeh stood up and kissed her father. He said, "Enjoy yourself, Daskele. You're a good girl, like your mother. You remind me of her, sometimes."

Daskeh thought of the framed photograph of her mother that hung above the dark sideboard in the apartment. To the girl, her mother was a pretty stranger in a lace blouse buttoned up to the chin. A woman with a heavy coil of black hair arranged in a knot at the nape of her neck, and solemn, light eyes.

"I wish I had known her. I wish I could be pretty, like her."

"To me, you are beautiful." Eli kissed his daughter. "And she, where she is, in heaven, is proud of you. Proud that at eleven years old you look after me, and work in the shop, and help your aunt at home." Tears began to film Eli's eyes.

Daskeh said quickly, "I must go now, Father. Take care of yourself until tonight."

"Go in peace, child," said Eli.

Daskeh walked through the shop and into the street. The light, striking sparks from the yellow stones all around her, dazzled her eyes. It was springtime already. Soon, on the almond tree in the courtyard of the house across the street, there would be blossoms. Daskeh walked up the hill, along winding sidewalks of smooth, flat stones. From somewhere in the distance came the sound of the guns, but Daskeh hardly heard them. She was thinking how many thousands of times she must have followed this same way home, through streets with high walls close together, full of secret places and unexpected gardens behind half-open wooden doors. Somewhere, beyond the apartment, was the Jaffa Road. Somewhere, there were shops, cafés and movies to which she never went.

My life is always the same, she thought, the shop and the apartment, the apartment and the shop. Nothing different ever happens. I see only family and customers. I have some pretty dresses, but who wears pretty dresses to wrap up sugar rations? I wish I could have stayed in school. I wish Father could afford to pay someone to work in the shop instead of me. Danny is my only friend, really. He's funny, like a little animal, quiet, with furry, soft hair. He's only ten, and he knits in the shelter at night, even though he's a boy. The sound of the guns and the shells frightens him. He's nice.

Daskeh walked on. Silent, pale men with long sidelocks of hair, wearing black frock coats and fur hats, passed her on their way to the synagogue. Small children were playing on the pavement, playing with stones or old pine cones left over from last year. Once upon a time, walking down this street on a Friday afternoon, you could smell the food cooking, all ready for the Sabbath. Once upon a time, this was the best part of the week, preparing for the day of rest. Daskeh made a list in her head of what she would have liked to make this afternoon, if there were no siege and all the food in the world to eat. An apple strudel. Aunt Pnina could roll the dough, thought Daskeh, and I would slice apples into half-moon shapes, and chop the nuts and sprinkle the sugar and cinnamon, and eat more raisins than went into the cake. Then we'd roll the whole thing up in the stretchy dough, Aunt Pnina at one end and me at the other, and put it into the oven to bake. I forgot the milk. I have to dip my fingers in the milk and stroke the top of the strudel, so that it comes out brown and shiny. And I have to make little slits in the dough for the air to come out. It's a long time since we baked.

Grinding for meatballs was good, too. Aunt Pnina used to sit down for a cup of tea while Daskeh did it all by herself, turning the handle of the silvery grinder with one hand and feeding things into its wide mouth with the other. She used to make different-colored worms squash out of the little holes and into the bowl. Orange carrot worms, and pearly onion worms, and pink meaty worms. Bread went into the grinder, too, and parsley and garlic: white and green-spotted worms. Then Aunt Pnina (who always managed to finish her tea just as the last morsel squished its way out) added an egg and salt, and mixed all the different colors up with a wooden spoon. Then she rolled the mixture into little balls and fried them in the big black frying pan, and put them into a white dish decorated with blue, long-legged birds.

Daskeh came out of her daydream and waved to her aunt, who was standing on the balcony of the apartment. Every day, she stood there and waited. Watching. A little afraid. Every day, Daskeh waved from the same place, and Aunt Pnina, relieved that the short walk was nearly over, happy that Daskeh was nearly home safe, waved back from the third floor.

The building had thick walls, and Daskeh shivered in the chilly, gray entrance hall. At night this place, with numbered boxes attached to one wall, became the shelter. All the families from all the apartments gathered there with blankets and candles when the firing from the guns grew louder. Daskeh ran up the stairs.

"There you are, then!" Aunt Pnina was standing at the door. "Come in, Daskele, and give me a big hug, and then we'll start work."

Daskeh hugged her aunt, pleased at the comfortable shape of her, sniffing the clean apron that, like the shop, seemed haunted by food smells from the past. Aunt Pnina's hair was tucked out of sight under a blue scarf, and the skin around her eyes became creased when she smiled. "Every wrinkle a sorrow, Daskele," she used to say. Daskeh would answer, "But you're not even old!" and Aunt Pnina would laugh. They went in together.

Everything that Daskeh loved was here. The can in the wardrobe, rattling with thousands of jewel-slippery buttons, the shawls to dress up in, and the white cupboard full of Aunt Pnina's shoes. Aunt Pnina was vain about her tiny feet. "Aristocratic feet," she called them. "Like a duchess." There were thirty pairs of shoes in the white cupboard, and they fitted Daskeh now, but when she was very small, three or four years old, she had clomped around for hours around the tiled floors, pretending to be a lady.

The best part of the apartment was the balcony.

You could sit there on a Friday evening, with all the work done, and look at the domes and towers and roofs of the gray-and-golden city spread around, and watch for the setting sun to mark the beginning of the Sabbath. On this balcony, there were cactus plants in squat, red pots. In the days when you could buy cucumbers in the market, Aunt Pnina used to pickle them in salty water and leave them in the sun in tall glass jars, where they floated in the milky, pale-green liquid like dead things. But how sharp and salty and good they tasted with potato pancakes, or hard-boiled eggs, or chopped liver—with almost anything. The floor of the balcony was made of square, honey-colored tiles. Each square had the shape of a flower cut into it. The tiles were unglazed, and caught and held the sunlight and the warmth. In the summer, in very hot weather, they were still warm to touch long after darkness had fallen.

"We'll set the table first," said Aunt Pnina, "and then go and see what's in the kitchen to eat."

Daskeh folded the oilcloth (patterned with red flowers and all the way from America) and put it away in a drawer of the sideboard. Aunt Pnina brought the Sabbath cloth from the cupboard in the bedroom. It was made of white linen, with white embroidery all around the edge. They spread it over the table.

Daskeh put the glasses on the table and said, "There—it's finished, Aunt Pnina."

"Good girl. Now come. Siege or no siege, the Sabbath will soon be here. We'll see what we can find to put in the old tin can."

They went into the kitchen. The tin can, which many years ago had held a few gallons of kerosene, was balanced on top of a little gas stove. Before the siege, all the Sabbath food used to be packed into the tin can with great care, and wedged firmly with dishtowels. Then a small flame was lit on the little gas stove, and the food would keep warm all through Friday night and Saturday, when cooking was forbidden. The coffee and tea in bottles were lukewarm by Saturday morning, the whites of the hard-boiled eggs were baked to a pale brown, and the yolks had faded to the color of moonlight.

"I wonder how long it will be before we have brown eggs again," said Daskeh.

"If an egg came to me covered in polka dots, I

would rejoice and sing," said Aunt Pnina. "But instead of eggs tonight, I have a special treat. A can of sardines. And I will make some kind of pancake, though how it will taste without eggs, I don't know. . . ."

"I'll open the can," Daskeh said, "and I won't spill a drop of the oil."

FRIDAY NIGHT

Outside the circle of candlelight, there was nothing but darkness and the rattle of the guns. The shelter was crowded. Daskeh sat next to Danny on the step and watched the faces, changed by the yellow light into masks full of black shadows that grew and shrank as the flames trembled. Mrs. Sirkis from the second floor was moaning again.

"Listen to them," she said, "just listen. It's coming from the direction of Barclay's Bank tonight, I can tell. That's where the fighting is now. They're shelling the Bank. And my poor diamonds, locked up there, what will become of them? My lovely diamonds . . ."

"Madam," said Grandfather Gluck, "if you give the diamonds to me, put them in my name, it would be the greatest pleasure in the world for me to worry about them. Nothing I'd like better."

Mrs. Sirkis promptly forgot her anguish and snapped, "You, Mr. Gluck, have no respect for property!"

"Because, madam, I have no property to respect. Your diamonds would be very good for me altogether."

Mrs. Sirkis sucked her teeth loudly, and folded her lips over them. There was nothing more to say.

Danny was knitting, frowning at the needles, shutting out of his ears every noise but their peaceful clicking. From time to time, an armored truck thundered by on the road outside, past the stone wall that blocked off the entrance to the apartments. Big, square monsters, these armored cars, with lamps for eyes. The lamps made rapid tracks of light along the walls as the trucks drove by, and Danny stopped knitting, holding himself stiffly until they had gone.

"What's that, Danny?" said Daskeh, "that you're making now? It's very pretty."

"A scarf for winter."

"You made a scarf before."

Silence. Then: "I only know how to make scarves."

"I think you're very clever to be able to make anything. I've tried. My fingers turn into wooden clothespins. Aunt Pnina is desperate. Maybe if I watch you . . ."

"I have to go slowly. There's not so much wool left."

"I can give you some. We unpicked a shawl the other day. Aunt Pnina thought the colors would encourage me."

"Did they?"

"No. I felt like crying. It was as if she were un-picking a rainbow. Anyway, if I give you the wool, you could knit it up again, couldn't you?"

"Thanks, Daskeh." The tapping of his needles was lost in a long and very close-sounding burst of gunfire. "That was very near us, wasn't it?"

"Are you scared?"

"No. Yes. Yes, I am. Aren't you?"

"Yes, a little. But we're safe here, you know. The walls are thick. And we're all together."

"It's not only us . . ." said Danny.

"Who, then?"

"Them. The others. Everyone who's fighting on both sides. In danger."

"Don't think of it now, Danny. Look, look at all the others, playing chess, reading books, some even sleeping. Listen, let me tell you what we had tonight. You'll never guess."

"What?"

"Sardines. A whole can. One sardine each, and the last one divided into three parts. It's very difficult to cut a sardine into three bits the same size. Where the tail is, it gets narrow, so you have to have a longer piece there, and a short piece up at the top where the fish is quite fat. My father spent ages carving it up and spooning out all the oil. It was heavenly. I licked the plate. I really did. Every drop."

"We ate our can last week," said Danny, "but I still remember how it tasted."

A voice whispered from the darkness: "Children, come. Come. I have something for you. Something good. Daskeh, Danny, come to me."

Daskeh hesitated. She knew who it was—Mrs. Birnbaum from the first floor. Dirty clothes, and fingers like the claws of an ancient bird. Mrs. Birnbaum, who watched the street all day from her balcony and talked to herself. Daskeh was a little afraid of her.

"Let's go, Danny. She can't hurt us. My father is here, and your mother. What can she do? Anyway, she might really have something good for us."

The children stood up and stepped over bodies and stretched-out legs until they came to the darkest corner of the shelter. Mrs. Birnbaum's eyes glittered in the candlelight. She put out a claw and took Daskeh's hand.

"Take, girl, take. It's for you. What do I need it for?"

"Thank you, Mrs. Birnbaum," said Daskeh. Danny said nothing. Daskeh could feel something hard, wrapped in paper, against her palm, as the claw held her hand imprisoned.

"Enjoy them in good health," said the old woman. "Sieges are for old women like me, and not for growing children, isn't that so?"

"Yes," said Danny, "and thank you very much."

Back in their place on the step, Daskeh opened

the bit of crumpled paper.

"Aniseed balls!" she breathed. "How beautiful! How marvelous! Four. Two each. Oh, lovely! Here's your share."

"Maybe we should each have one now, and keep one for tomorrow?" said Danny.

"Are you crazy? What for? Ooh, I'm going to suck and suck them very gently. They'll last for ages. Maybe all night." Daskeh put one into her mouth and closed her eyes.

"They change color," said Danny after a while, and Daskeh took her candy out to have a look at it. It had been brown, and was now orange. It turned purple, pink, and green, and when all the colors were gone, only a tiny white ball the size of a pea was left. Danny sucked his to the end, but Daskeh grew impatient and crunched the pale, sugary heart to powder with her teeth. Then she sighed happily and began to suck the second aniseed ball.

Someone was singing.

"It's Rina Gluck, Danny, listen. Singing to her baby. Did you have that song when you were little?" Daskeh joined in, soothed by the rhythm of the words:

"Yak
Yaksen trak,
Yaksen traksen traksen trony.
Tsipka,
Tsipka dripka,
Tsipka dripka yampamponi.
Yak and Tsipka,
Yaksen trak and Tsipka dripka,
Yaksen traksen traksen trony and Tsipka dripka
yampamponi."

"I know that," said Danny. "I used to think that they were people. Boys and girls. Then when they grew up, Yak married Tsipka, Yaksen trak married Tsipka dripka, like that. Then the two with very long names got married at the end."

"That's a good idea. I never thought of that." Daskeh leaned against the wall with a cushion under her head, and sucked at her candy until she fell asleep.

Much later, the silence woke her, and the cold. The candles were out, and in the metal-gray light that filled the shelter, she could see the lumps of bodies bunched under blankets and hear the muffled snores of old men. No more guns. Beside her,

~
77

Danny lay curled up like a cat, clutching his scarf. Daskeh shook him and whispered in his ear.

"Danny. Wake up, Danny. They're asleep. It's morning. Wake up." Danny opened his eyes, awake at once.

"It's all right," said Daskeh gently. "It's daytime. No guns, no trucks. Let's go up on the roof."

"We're not allowed to."

"But everyone is asleep. They'll never know. We won't stay long. Listen to the snoring! Just be careful not to step on anybody."

Danny still looked worried, but he followed Daskeh out of the shelter and up and up and up onto the flat roof of the building.

"Why do we come here?" he asked. "There's nothing but boring old water tanks and stupid lines of wash."

"I like it. You can see quite far. Over there, there's the King David Hotel and the YMCA tower and the hills, and all the streets I've hardly ever been in, the streets I don't know."

"Where's Rehavia? Which way?"

"There, I think." Daskeh pointed toward the horizon. "It's very grand, that part of town. They have trees in the streets, with railings around

~

them. I went there once."

"It's cold here," said Danny. "Can't we go back?"

"Don't be such a baby."

The sky was the color of pearls, the color of doves, and the walls of the city were pale in the dawn, like good butter. Daskeh said, "I feel as if I could walk for miles and never come back. I feel as if I could fly away, miles away, away from the shop, and this building, away to some strange place that no one has ever been to."

"That's silly," said Danny. "There are no strange places out there. Only the rest of Jerusalem."

"Shut up. What do you know about it? I'm just bored, that's all. I want to see something different. What's silly about that?"

"Nothing, I suppose."

"You suppose. . . . What do you want, then? Just to stay here knitting every day? Don't you ever want to go somewhere else?"

Danny sat down on an upturned tin tub. "There's somewhere I want to go to."

"Where?"

"There. In Rehavia."

"What's there?"

"It's where my mother's aunt lives. Aunt Simha, her name is."

"Then why don't you go, if she's family? Why don't you go with your parents?"

"They don't visit her anymore," said Danny. "They had a quarrel. Something stupid."

"Is she nice, this aunt of yours?"

"She's funny. Strange. She used to give me cakes made out of sesame seeds, all stuck together. They were diamond-shaped."

"Well, you won't get those now. No sugar, so no cakes."

"She's fat. She wears about twenty gold bracelets on each arm. She hasn't got very much hair."

"Could you find the way?"

"I don't know. I've never tried."

"Well, do you know the name of the street?"

"Yes," said Danny. "Ussishkin Street. And I know the number, twenty-two."

"Then we could ask."

"Yes, we could. Do you want to go?"

"They wouldn't let us go alone," said Daskeh, "and your parents have quarreled."

Danny smiled. "We don't have to tell them. We could just go."

Daskeh felt a fluttering in her stomach, like a bird. Fear and pleasure mixed together. They would run away, no one would know where they were. . . .

"We'd have to arrange it very carefully." Daskeh sat down next to Danny on the tub, and began to plan. "Listen. Everyone must think we're with someone else. I'll tell my father I can't help in the shop because I have to help Aunt Pnina with something or other. Aunt Pnina will think I'm in the shop till five o'clock. Your mother goes out and gets her rations very early in the morning, so you can tell her I've asked you to keep me company behind the counter. She'll never know. No one will know. If we leave early enough, we'll be back long before it's dark."

"What a good plan. You are clever, Daskeh. I'd never have thought of all that. It'll be an adventure, won't it? When will we go?"

"Tuesday, I think. We'll talk about it again, don't worry. Come on, now. We must go down to the shelter. They'll be waking up soon."

~

They tiptoed down the stairs.

"See," said Daskeh. "What did I tell you? They're all still asleep."

"Eat it, Daskele. What are you staring at it for?" Aunt Pnina pointed to the teaspoonful of jam lying on the saucer. "It's full of sugar. To give you strength for the day."

Daskeh hardly heard her. Absentmindedly, she picked up the spoon, and licked the red stickiness very delicately with her tongue. Then she took a mouthful of water. If you managed it right, you could make the jam last until every drop of the water had gone.

"You're not with us today at all. Dreaming. It's not like you," said Aunt Pnina.

Daskeh looked across to the other end of the table. On the wall behind her aunt's head, she could see the colored zigzags of the cross-stitched wall hanging, like mountains from a country visited in dreams: orange, scarlet, brown and royal-blue peaks and valleys, green and yellow foothills at the bottom. This hanging, the size of a blanket, had always been there on the wall, and Daskeh had grown so used to it, she scarcely saw it anymore. But now, on this day, to prevent Aunt Pnina from noticing how excited she was, she said, "I was thinking about the cross-stitch mountains. Did you really make it? All by yourself?"

"How many times have I told you? A hundred? A thousand?"

"But tell it again. How old were you?"

"Seventeen. And beautiful. You wouldn't believe. With an eighteen-inch waist. Well, twenty inches, maybe. Look at me now. Many more inches around the waist, eh?" Aunt Pnina patted her stomach. "Well, my father and mother had arranged for me to marry a young man. He was from a good family. A religious family. But his parents had trouble persuading him to come and meet me. He was in love with someone else."

"Did he come in the end?"

"Yes, he came. And it was like Romeo and Juliet. One look at me, and that was that. The other girl was forgotten. The wedding was all arranged. I began to embroider that as a bedspread."

"Then what happened?"

"You see how the colors start bright and happy? Look, yellow and red and orange, and green, can you see?"

"Yes," said Daskeh.

"And have you seen this?" Aunt Pnina pointed to a band of black near the middle.

"That was when he died, wasn't it?"

"That's right. Poor Avram. Twenty years old. He looked so healthy, too. A most terrible fever took him. After I had finished the black bit, I left the blanket in the chest. I left it there for two years. Then when Leah was to be married, I took it out. I thought I'd finish it for her, and I did, but when the time came to give it to her, I couldn't part with it, so I put it up here. And here it still is. Maybe for you, when you are married. What do I need it for? Haven't we got enough problems without being sad about what's finished? You, you're like my own daughter, so you shall have it."

"How lovely, Aunt Pnina. Thank you. I haven't really looked at it for such a long time. It's beautiful. Like mountains, and blue sky right at the top."

"Come now, Daskele, it's time you went to the shop. Your father will be waiting."

"Yes," said Daskeh, and kissed her aunt good-bye. "I'll be back this evening. Have a good day, darling Aunt Pnina. I love you so much."

"What's this? What's this? All this love, so early in the morning! You are funny today, girl. I don't know what's the matter with you. Get along, now, or you'll be late."

Daskeh ran down the stairs and knocked on Danny's door. His mother opened it.

"Hello, Mrs. Rakov. Is Danny ready?"

"Yes, he's ready. Is it all right with your father that he should be in the shop all day? I meant to ask your father last night, but what with one thing and another . . ."

"Yes, it's fine," said Daskeh, smiling at Mrs. Rakov in her relief. What a narrow escape. If Mrs. Rakov had asked her father . . . Daskeh didn't like to think about it. "It'll be company for me."

Danny was standing behind his mother. He looked worried.

"Come, Danny. Daskeh's waiting." Mrs. Rakov put a paper bag into his hand. "Here's something for your lunch. Mr. Genzel has enough worries without having to feed you."

"What is it?" asked Danny.

"Nothing much. A couple of matzos, that's all, and a bit of cheese."

Daskeh smiled again, pleased at how well everything was turning out. Here was a picnic lunch provided for them. Yesterday, she had saved a cookie, and it lay now wrapped in paper, deep in the pocket of her brown cotton skirt. A feast.

"Good-bye, Mother," said Danny.

"Good-bye, Danny, be good. Don't be a trouble for Mr. Genzel."

"I won't, Mother," said Danny, and waved to her as he followed Daskeh down the stairs.

Outside, in the street, Daskeh said: "Let's see if all the balconies are clear. We don't want anyone to see us going the wrong way. Is Mrs. Birnbaum there?" They looked. Every balcony was empty.

"Right," said Daskeh. "Now run, and don't stop till we get to the hospital."

She started off down the hill, with Danny running behind her. They came, panting, to a low wall with railings on top of it, and leaned against it to rest.

"Let's cross to the other side of the street," said Danny.

"Why? What's wrong with this side?"

"I don't like all the sick people on the sidewalk in their robes."

"Those are the ones that aren't sick, silly. The sick ones are in bed. These are the ones who are getting better, and need fresh air. They haven't got a garden, so they sit outside on the sidewalk sometimes, that's all."

"Please let's cross. They look sick and yellow and old. Please."

Daskeh sighed. "All right, I suppose so," she said, and she took Danny's hand as they crossed the street and continued down the hill.

They passed lines of people with buckets in their hands, lining up for their ration of water. Long, tight curls of barbed wire lay in the road, and there were soldiers with angry-looking rifles slung over their shoulders. Nobody took any notice of the thin girl in the brown skirt and black stockings and the boy almost running to keep up with her. Then the children stopped to look into the window of a jeweler's shop. The jeweler saw them for a moment from behind his counter, and a thought like a leaf blown by the wind flew into his head: What are those children doing, alone, here in the middle of town, in the middle of a war? But just then, his wife screeched for something from upstairs, and the man left his counter to see what she wanted. By the time he came back, the children had gone. He worried about them from time to time for the rest of the morning.

"My feet are hurting."

"Come on, Danny, you can't stop there. Look, it's not much further. This *is* the street, isn't it?"

"Yes. That's the house there. With the pointed trees in the garden, and the blue flowers hanging over the wall."

"Then what are we waiting for?"

"I don't know." Danny looked down to where the toe of his shoe was scratching patterns in the dust. "Maybe she's out. Maybe she won't want to see us. Maybe we shouldn't have come."

"It's a fine time you've chosen, haven't you, to say all this? Now that we're practically sitting on her doorstep? Why didn't you think of it before? This was all your idea."

Danny's eyes filled with tears. "Don't be angry,

Daskeh. I just . . . I don't know, I feel nervous."

"Well, stop feeling nervous this minute. And stop sniveling. You're nothing but a crybaby."

"Don't be angry, Daskeh. Make friends. Please."

"I *am* friends," shouted Daskeh, "but you're so silly. Here. Take my hanky and blow your nose." Danny rubbed his nose obediently. "Now. Stand up straight, and put a smile on that face, for once. We're going visiting. Follow me." Daskeh strode off toward the gate. Danny walked beside her, dragging his feet. As they stood in front of the door, Daskeh suddenly felt nervous herself. She looked at Danny's white face, and nearly, so nearly took him by the hand, and ran away. You're not much braver than he is, Hadassah Genzel, she told herself. Ring that bell. And she put her finger on it before she could change her mind.

The door was opened by an enormously fat woman. Daskeh saw the gold bracelets on her arms, just as Danny had said. This was Aunt Simha. Nobody said anything for a while. Aunt Simha looked at Daskeh, then at Danny, then at Daskeh again. Danny said, "Don't you recognize me, Aunt Simha? It's Danny Rakov."

The old woman clapped her hand over her mouth and stared. Then she shouted, "Danny, my darling! Such a long time . . . What a big boy. How you've grown!" and she almost buried the boy in the flapping pieces of lace in which she was draped. Danny struggled for air after a few moments, and his aunt released him.

"This is my friend, Daskeh. She—"

"Don't stand here, children. Daskeh. So good to see a friend of Danny's. Come into the house. Come and sit. Have you walked?"

"We walked all the way," said Daskeh, but Aunt Simha was no longer listening. Like a fat butterfly, she had settled on another topic of conversation.

"Are you hungry? You must be hungry. Children are always hungry, isn't that right? Let me see now, what do I have for you? Not much, these days, but sit, and I will bring."

Daskeh and Danny sat on a plush-covered sofa. The shutters were closed, and bars of sunlight striped the carpet. Aunt Simha was making clattering noises in the kitchen.

"Is your aunt very rich?" whispered Daskeh.

"Yes, I think so," said Danny. "I think she's a bit

of a miser. That's what my mother says. She wouldn't give them money to buy a shop, or something like that. How did you know she was rich?"

"The carpet is all red and silky. And look at the shiny copper things all over the place. And velvet curtains. They look a little dusty, but aren't they grand? It's like something in a book."

Aunt Simha waddled back into the room, carrying a brass tray.

"Danny," she said, "be a good boy and put that little table in front of the sofa. See what your aunty has found for you, my love."

The table was inlaid with a mosaic of mother-of-pearl.

"It's beautiful," said Daskeh.

"Beautiful things I have," said Aunt Simha sadly. "Only happiness I lack. But today, such a wonderful surprise, to see my darling Danny again. Eat now, children. See, I have some sesame seed cakes."

Daskeh closed her eyes. It's a dream, she thought. In a moment I shall wake up and find myself spooning tea into little pieces of newspaper in my father's shop. When she opened her eyes, the diamond-shaped cakes were still there.

"Take, Daskeh. Don't be shy," said Aunt Simha. The two children began to eat and went on eating until the gaps between their teeth were full of tiny seeds, their mouths sweet with the taste of the cakes. Aunt Simha nodded from her chair, her chins wobbling with pleasure. She said: "Now you will have tea. With mint leaves. And sugar." She went into the kitchen again.

"How wonderful that was!" said Daskeh, chasing the last few crumbs around the plate with a sticky finger. "And tea with sugar . . . What about the mint? Will she mind if I don't have mint?"

"It's what they drink in Morocco. That's where she was born. Mint tea tastes lovely."

"I think I'd rather have lemon, but I suppose it would be rude to ask, after she's been so nice."

"Aren't you glad I thought of coming?" said Danny.

Daskeh laughed. "Danny Rakov! You wanted to go back. Remember? It's thanks to me we're here at all."

The mint tea was delicious. I must tell Aunt Pnina about it, thought Daskeh, and for a moment felt a longing to be at home with her aunt. What would she be doing? What would she say if she ever found out about this visit? Daskeh shivered and looked up at the clock. Whatever happened, they must not arrive home late. Aunt Pnina was probably sponging the black-and-yellow tiled floors, or maybe ironing . . . Her father was in the shop, dealing alone with all the customers pleading, wheedling, sure that Genzel was keeping some morsel of food from them. They would try to pry into the back room to see what treasures were hidden there. Her father wouldn't know how to manage. Daskeh chuckled to herself as she remembered the look on Mrs. Meltzer's face. . . . I certainly lost my temper with her . . . dragged her behind the counter and opened every drawer to show her it was empty, then banged it shut! And I yelled at her, too. It's a good thing Father was out of the shop. He would have made me take some of our rations over to her house. I would have had to apologize. . . .

Aunt Simha talked incessantly. About the siege, about the old days, about her youth, about how sickly Danny had been as a baby. Pointed silver hands made their way around the clock, and the bars of light lengthened across the carpet.

"Aunt Simha," said Danny, after Daskeh had

kicked him on the shin and pointed at the clock, "we have to go home now."

"So soon? You only just came. Why do you have to go so soon? What's the hurry?"

"It's been really lovely," said Daskeh. "We have enjoyed it. And thank you for the tea and the beautiful sesame cakes. We have to be home before five o'clock, and it's quite a long way."

"But your mother won't worry, Danny, if she knows you're with me," said Aunt Simha.

"No," said Danny quickly, "but we must go. Daskeh has to help her aunt prepare supper."

"Well, you will come again soon. Both of you. Won't you? Please?"

Aunt Simha looked so sad that the children said "Yes."

"Good," said Aunt Simha, and struggled out of her chair. "Now, I'm going to give you both something to take home. A present. Come with me. I have it in the kitchen."

On the table, lying in a saucer, were two eggs. Real eggs. Aunt Simha picked them up and wrapped them in a clean cloth.

"Take care of them, now. Don't break them."

"Are you sure, Aunty?" said Danny. "Don't you need them?"

"Do I look as if I need food?" Aunt Simha laughed. "You need it more. Have one each. Have it for supper, and think of me when you eat it. And remember to come again."

Daskeh took the eggs and held them gently in her hands. Aunt Simha covered her for a moment in waves of material as she kissed her good-bye. Then Danny disappeared for a long time under the draperies. Aunt Simha watched the children going down the road until they turned the corner. Then she started crying quietly, dabbing her eyes with a stray corner of lace. From far away came the sound of the guns.

"I'll have mine boiled," said Daskeh. "Soft-boiled."

"I think I'll have an omelette."

"Or fried is nice," said Daskeh, "but it's a waste of oil. Boiled is best. My arms are hurting from carrying them so carefully. I feel as if I'm holding a baby."

"Let me have them for a bit," said Danny.

"You'd probably drop them."

"I wouldn't."

"You would."

"Wouldn't."

"All right. Here. Take them for a while. But if you drop them, I'll kill you. I will, really." Daskeh gave Danny the eggs. Then she bent down to take a stone out of her shoe. Danny walked on.

There was no one in the street. As Daskeh ran to catch up with Danny, he shouted out, "Daskeh! What are you hitting me for? What have I done?" and dropped the eggs. They burst out of the cloth as they fell to the ground, and the yolks mingled with the yellow dust on the pavement. Daskeh couldn't even open her mouth to cry out. She stared at the smashed eggs and felt a scream of rage rising in her throat. She could see nothing but the spreading pools of yolk and crushed fragments of shell. Then—

"Daskeh, I'm bleeding," said Danny.

Daskeh looked at him. He held out his hand. It was streaked with blood, sticky with it. How? Why? What was that he had shouted out? Something about her hitting him. She hadn't touched him. All the warmth rushed out of her heart. She opened her mouth, but no sound came. Thudding noises filled her head. Danny had been shot. Had there been guns? Yes, there they were, still, tap-tapping in the distance. On the wall, just behind the children, there was a bullet hole. A stray bullet, it must have been, to have come so far. A freak. Hurting poor Danny like that!

At last, Daskeh said, "Sit down, Danny. Let me see it. Where is it?"

"Here, on my shoulder."

Daskeh tore Danny's shirt from around the wound, and looked. All the blood made her feel sick, but she could see that Danny was biting his lip trying not to cry, and she knew that he would if she looked at all worried.

"It's not so bad," she said. "Just a lot of blood. A graze from the bullet, that's all. Like the kind of cut you get from a bad fall. I'll clean it up. Can you help me to take your shirt off?"

Together they took off the shirt, and Daskeh mopped up the blood. Then she took her own handkerchief and tied it as well as she could around Danny's shoulder, over the wound.

"There, now. We'll hurry to get home. I suppose we're going to have to tell them everything.

There's no hiding something like this." Daskeh felt angry with Danny for a moment for spoiling the smooth working of her plan, and being stupid enough to stand in the way of a stray bullet, and drop the eggs. Just then, as if he had had the same thought, Danny started crying, howling and sobbing and weeping for his mother. Daskeh forgot her anger and sat down beside him on the sidewalk, holding his head against her shoulder.

"Don't cry, Danny. Be brave. I know it hurts. But we'll soon be home. I'll help you. Don't worry. You'll be with your mother very soon."

"But the eggs . . . I dropped the eggs. You said you'd kill me if I dropped them. You were going to have a boiled egg tonight."

"Never mind about me killing you and boiled eggs," said Daskeh, suddenly aware of how near Danny's shoulder was to his head, how nearly he had escaped. "Stand up now, if you can."

"I don't think I can, really." Danny spoke snuffily, through his tears.

"It's lucky you're so small, then, isn't it, if I'm going to have to carry you all the way—and lucky you had the sense not to get shot at in Rehavia."

Daskeh lifted the boy onto her hip, as she had

seen mothers do with small children. He was not as heavy as a big box of groceries, but she had never had to carry a box of groceries so far. Danny was still crying, but more quietly now.

The children were silent as Daskeh struggled up the hill. Danny's shoulder had begun to bleed again. She could see the hospital now, with the old, yellow people on the pavement outside. Hospital. Daskeh nearly dropped Danny in her relief.

"Danny, I'm going to take you to the hospital. They'll put something on your shoulder to make it better. Also, your mother and Aunt Pnina and my father won't be so angry. They'll see that we know what to do, how to take care of ourselves."

"I'm not going in there," shouted Danny. "I'm frightened. I want my mother."

"Well, you can't get to your mother without me, and I'm taking you to the hospital first, so you can howl all you like."

Daskeh pushed her way past the people lying about in the entrance and dropped Danny onto the lap of a startled nurse in a white dress.

"He's been hit by a bullet," she said. "Could you have a look, please?"

The nurse hurried to get a doctor, and they

began to carry Danny down the corridor. Daskeh followed them.

"There's really no need for you to come, dear," said the nurse. "He'll be out in a minute, as soon as we bandage the wound."

"I'm coming," said Daskeh. "I'm supposed to be looking after him. He'll be scared if I don't come."

"Let her come," said the doctor. "It doesn't matter."

Daskeh watched as they cleaned the wound and put some ointment on it, and a bandage.

The nurse talked to Daskeh as she worked.

"Where do you live?"

"Not far. Number nine, Chancellor Street. Just up the road."

"We haven't got an ambulance at the moment, but if you wait, maybe we can get one to take you home."

"Oh, no," said Daskeh, "thank you." (Aunt Pnina, seeing an ambulance from the balcony, oh, never, never!) "I'll carry him. He's very light."

"Is he your brother?"

"He's my friend. He lives in the apartment downstairs. We went to visit his aunt. We didn't tell anyone we were going, you see, so we don't want them to be frightened by an ambulance."

"Yes, I see. Very well. There's nothing very wrong with his shoulder. You tied it up very nicely, young lady. It'll be better in two or three days, but tell his mother he should be in bed at least twenty-four hours."

"Yes, I will. Thank you very much. Come on, Danny." Daskeh picked him up, and walked out of the hospital.

Aunt Pnina just happened to be on the balcony and looking down the street, when she saw what was unmistakably Daskeh coming toward the building from the wrong direction. Carrying Danny! Why weren't they coming from the shop? Why were they coming so early? Danny seemed to be asleep. Why wasn't he wearing a shirt? Something was very wrong indeed. Aunt Pnina asked herself no more questions. She ran to the front door of the apartment, and down the stairs to the street. She was coming out of the entrance just as Daskeh reached it.

"Daskele, Danny, what's happened? Why are you carrying him? Where's your father? Why aren't you in the shop?"

~
101

"Oh, Aunt Pnina, I'm so glad, so happy to see you. Danny was grazed by a bullet. We didn't go to the shop. We went to visit his aunt. We didn't want to tell you. Not his aunt, his mother's aunt . . ."

"Whose aunt doesn't matter. Why are we standing talking in the street with a hurt child? Come, I'll carry him now, and we'll take him up to his mother. How far have you carried him?"

"I don't know. Quite far."

Aunt Pnina smiled and said nothing.

"I took him to the hospital down there, and they put a bandage on. He's to stay in bed for twenty-four hours."

Outside Danny's apartment, Aunt Pnina said to Daskeh, "You go on up. I'll explain it all to Mrs. Rakov. You've had enough trouble for one day. The door's open."

Daskeh ran up the stairs to the third floor. She went into the empty apartment and sat down. Home. She was home. She looked at the cross-stitch hanging on the wall, the lines of colored mountains, the shapes of unknown lands and hidden valleys, and began to tremble, suddenly cold.

When Aunt Pnina came up from talking to Mrs. Rakov, Daskeh took one look at her aunt and burst into tears.

"Oh, Aunt Pnina, what if something dreadful had happened to him?"

Aunt Pnina sat down next to Daskeh and put her arm gently around the girl's shoulders.

"Nothing dreadful happened. Just a graze. It could have been a fall. When your father was Danny's age, he broke his nose falling out of a tree. These things happen."

"But we ran away. . . . We never told anyone where we were going. . . ."

"That's something else, Daskele. Why didn't you tell anyone? That was foolish. And danger-ous."

"Because you would have stopped us. You wouldn't have let us go alone. And I was so bored. So tired of the same thing every day, the same places, the same people, everything always the same. I never go anywhere different. I never see new places. I wanted . . . I don't know . . . I just wanted to run away for a little while. I'm sorry."

"Sorry you don't have to be," said Aunt Pnina.

"When I was young I was just the same. I remember, when I embroidered those mountains, imagining strange countries, oh, marvelous places beyond the top of every hill. When I was young, and, if I'm honest, even now, sometimes, that was where I wanted to be—somewhere else."

"Then you aren't angry with me?"

"It's too late for that. And you're in no fit state to be shouted at, and I'm so thankful to God that neither you nor Danny was badly hurt, that I feel like singing for joy. But instead of singing, I'll make tea and we will talk about all the places we will go together. When the fighting is over. Full of bullet holes, like a sieve, I'm not ready to be, even for you."

Daskeh laughed. "What did you tell Mrs. Rakov?"

"Mrs. Rakov? She wasn't in a mood to listen to me, poor thing. But she said, 'Thank God Daskeh was there. What would have happened without her?'"

"He would have been safe at home all the time, that's what," said Daskeh. "But on the other hand, he wouldn't have had those cakes."

"What cakes?"

~
104

"Sesame-seed cakes, we had. And tea with mint. And sugar. It was beautiful. Mrs. Rakov's aunt is very rich and very fat."

"Come and tell me, while I make the tea," said Aunt Pnina, and Daskeh went with her aunt into the kitchen.

TUESDAY NIGHT

There was a mattress in the shelter for Danny. Daskeh was sitting on it, looking at Danny, who was leaning against the pillows.

"Does it hurt?" she wanted to know.

"Not badly, really. But I can't knit."

"Never mind. I've got my wool all ready for you as soon as you want it. Was your mother angry?"

"No. I was surprised. She says she's going to take me to Aunt Simha's again, when I'm better. She says it's time the quarrel was made up. You can come too. Maybe we'll get some eggs again. I'm sorry about the eggs, Daskeh."

"You're stupid. Who cares about the eggs? You should go to sleep now, or you won't get better quickly."

"Sing me a song."

"Which one?"

"Any song. A lullaby."

So Daskeh sang.

When she stopped singing, Danny was asleep. Daskeh curled up at his feet and closed her eyes. I'm so tired, she thought, I'll be asleep very soon. But she lay awake for a long time with her eyes shut, listening to the waves of voices murmuring in the corners of the shelter, listening to the pounding of the guns.

DREAMS OF FIRE.
1950.

One Wednesday afternoon in August, Danny lay on top of his bed and thought he knew exactly what it felt like to be a loaf of bread, baking on a hot shelf in the oven. The shutters had been closed to keep out the worst of the heat, but thin stripes of sunlight always managed to creep in, and those stripes now lay across Danny's bare legs. I look like a zebra, he thought, and in a minute I'll have to face Daskeh. It's nearly time for music class.

Danny and Daskeh took piano lessons from Mrs. Strauss, who lived in Rehavia, and on Wednesday afternoons they went to her apartment together. Danny had his lesson first and Daskeh waited for him, then she had her lesson and he waited for her and they came home together. It was a very satisfactory arrangement. He sighed. She'll be angry with me, he thought. She'll have to go all by herself, and she'll be annoyed with me. Tears prickled behind his eyes and he blinked them away. Everything was bad enough without adding tears to it. Tears would make everything worse. Someone knocked at the apartment door, and Danny heard his mother opening it and talking to Daskeh. What Daskeh said he couldn't hear, because she was still on the landing outside.

"Danny's not very well," his mother was saying. "I don't know exactly what. . . . I can't find anything wrong, but he doesn't sleep. Sometimes I hear him walking about in the middle of the night. There's no getting two words out of him— well, you know how stubborn he can be. Can't let him go to music today—I'm sure Mrs. Strauss will understand. What? Really? Yes, I suppose so. If you've got the time. Come in for a moment. I'm sure he'll be happy to see you."

Oh, no, thought Danny, and he turned away from the door of his room to face the wall. She's coming in. She's going to talk to me. She's going to ask me. I can't bear it. What will I tell her?

"Hello, Danny," said Daskeh. She came in and immediately sat down beside him on the bed. "What's wrong with you? Why aren't you coming with me? We could have a doughnut at Café Allenby."

"Nothing's wrong."

"Then why are you in bed?"

"I'm not in bed. It's too hot. I'm on the bed."

Daskeh sighed. "You know exactly what I mean. Are you sick?"

"Not really."

"Have you got a headache?"

"No."

"Stomachache?"

"No."

"Earache?"

Danny turned around, exasperated. "Since when have you become a doctor? I'm *not* sick. I just . . ." He fell silent, and looked away.

"Just what?"

"I just haven't been sleeping very well."

"I know. Your mother says she hears you walking around in the night. But why not?"

"I stop myself."

"What?"

"I stop myself from sleeping. That's why I walk around." Danny suddenly seemed absorbed in a tiny speck on his pillow.

"I'm fed up with this!" Daskeh stood up. "Stop pretending that pillow's the most fascinating thing you've ever seen in your life and tell me why you're being so stupid. Tell me why you're making yourself sick on purpose. Tell me why you don't sleep. I've never heard of anyone doing anything like that before."

Danny said, "It's hard to explain. I don't want to sleep because I don't like the dreams I have when I do. Nightmares, that's what they are. I have nightmares every night about Bab-el-Waad."

It was Daskeh's turn to be silent. Bab-el-Waad was a village in the hills outside Jerusalem. In the 1948 war, a convoy of trucks had been ambushed and set on fire there, and now the rusting metal skeletons of those trucks stood among the rocks and trees as a memorial to all who had died during the attack. There was even a song about it, which you could hear almost every time you turned on the radio.

"Have you been to Bab-el-Waad?" Daskeh asked.

"I went with the Scouts, in the spring. And now I have nightmares all the time. One nightmare, really, because it's always the same. I'm in a truck, and it's standing on the side of the hill, and it starts burning. I can see flames creeping along the hood, toward me. I can feel the heat. I can see other trucks on fire all around me, and people are walking about and they're on fire too. Oh, it's horrible, Daskeh. I can't describe to you how horrible. Can you imagine what it must have been like to be trapped in one of those trucks? I can't get it out of my mind. It makes me so scared, Daskeh, that I'd rather just not sleep, but it's hard to keep awake sometimes. My eyes close up in the end all by themselves, and then the dreams start up all over again, as if they've been waiting on the insides of my eyelids, waiting for my eyes to close."

"I don't know what to say, Danny," said Daskeh. "'It's awful for you. Maybe if you talk about it a lot, then the nightmares will go away. That's what my father says."

"I can only tell you," said Danny. "Everyone at school would think I was a baby. They all think battles are wonderful, and soldiers are heroes who never get hurt. And everyone thinks we should be brave, us boys, just like grown-up soldiers. I'd never, ever tell any of them. Do you remember the victory parade through the streets when the war ended? How we stood on your balcony shouting and cheering and threw oranges down to the marching men? Do you remember how splendid the music sounded and how tall and strong all the soldiers looked? They looked as if they didn't know what fear was. I try to think about that, and not about Bab-el-Waad, and during the day it's easy."

"Danny, I have to go to music class now," said Daskeh. "I'll tell Mrs. Strauss you've got a stomachache. And I'll come and visit you again."

She waved to him from the door as she left the room.

Daskeh hurried to Rehavia, thinking about Danny. She had spoken with him for so long that there was no time to buy a doughnut. Perhaps his mother should get pills from the doctor to make him sleep. Should she tell Mrs. Strauss the truth? No, a stomachache sounded more reasonable, and besides, she'd promised Danny. Breathless from walking so quickly, Daskeh arrived at her piano teacher's building just as another pupil was leaving. Mrs. Strauss met her in the hall.

"And where is little Danny today?" she asked. Daskeh smiled, thinking how Danny would have hated to be called "little."

"He's not very well," she said. "He has a stomachache and sends you his apologies."

"In that case, we have a little extra time. Come into the salon and have a drink. My son Alex is there . . . you remember me telling you about him. It's so hot. I'm sure you need some refreshment." She bustled into the apartment, and Daskeh followed her.

～

She always felt enormous in Mrs. Strauss's apartment. It was full of tiny china ornaments in pale pastel colors balanced on shaky little wooden tables. The rugs were pale too, and all the furniture looked daintier and more flimsy than furniture is supposed to look, so that Daskeh never sat down on a chair without fearing that it would break. Mrs. Strauss (who was tiny and doll-like too, to go with her house) wore mauve dresses and had a bun perched right on top of her head. She wore the same black laced-up shoes all year round, and today Daskeh felt sweaty just thinking of them. Mrs. Strauss had magic fingers. That was what she told Daskeh, and Daskeh saw no reason to disbelieve her. When they were not racing up and down the keys of the piano, causing waterfalls and fountains of beautiful melodies to spill into every corner of the room, the magic fingers were spinning crochet mats as fine as spiders' webs to sit under the porcelain figurines of shepherdesses and young men in striped waistcoats and white wigs. Mrs. Strauss had lived in Israel since 1934, when she and her husband had fled from Germany, but her Hebrew was still very foreign-sounding.

"Please to call me Madame," she had said when Daskeh first went to her for lessons. "This is what I am used to."

Daskeh went into the living room, which Madame called "the salon." Mrs. Strauss said, "In one minute, I will be all for you, Daskeh. First I will go into the kitchen for the cold drink jug. A person can faint today, it is so hot. Please to meet my son, Alex. Alex, please to meet my pupil, Daskeh."

The salon was very dark, because the shutters were closed to keep out the sun. Daskeh could just see, though, the shape of a young man sitting on the hard, uncomfortable sofa. He stood up when his name was said.

"Hello," he said. "Come and sit down. This is the only room that's not like an oven. My mother will bring homemade lemonade, which is delicious."

Daskeh forgot her shyness at once. "I've heard such a lot about you, how you were the most gifted violinist for your age, playing in concerts when you were six, or was it five?"

Alex laughed. "You know how parents exaggerate. I don't think I was ever that good, and in any case . . . well, it doesn't matter. How about you? How long have you been learning to play the piano?"

"About four years."

"And are you good?"

"Not very good," said Daskeh, "but I like it. I especially like hearing Madame—I mean your mother—play the pieces for me. That's the best part."

It occurred to Daskeh as she spoke that Madame had been very quiet on the subject of her son for a very long time now. She tried to remember when was the last time she had heard something about him, and couldn't really bring it to mind. She said, "I think I thought you'd gone to Europe or something. I can't really recall."

Alex laughed. "Not Europe. I've been in the hospital. In fact, I live in Tel-Aviv. I'm visiting my mother now. Convalescing."

"Were you ill?" Daskeh peered through the gloom at him. He looked strong enough from what she could see.

"No, not ill. I was injured during the war. My arms . . . they were badly burned, so I've been in the hospital, having treatment. Of course, my hands and arms are not a pretty sight, but at least I still have them. My hands, I mean. And, more importantly, I'm alive."

At that moment, Mrs. Strauss called Daskeh for her lesson.

"I have to go now," she said. "It was lovely to meet you."

"I'm sure we'll meet again soon," said Alex. "I'm usually here in the afternoons."

"Daskeh! You are not concentrating! What has happened to your scales? Do you have fingers, or do you have instead sausages? Quick and delicate, please remember. Quick and delicate."

Daskeh took her hands off the keys and turned to Mrs. Strauss. She was struggling not to cry, but in spite of all her efforts, two tears were trickling down her cheeks toward her chin. She wiped them away with the backs of her hands.

"Child! Child! What have I said?" Mrs. Strauss was fluttery with remorse. "Please, not to cry on account of the clumsy scale. Please!"

"It's not the scales, Madame. It's Alex. I spoke to Alex in the salon, and I can't stop thinking about it . . . his hands. I look at my fingers and I see his, and I can't bear to think of it. You used to tell such stories of him playing the violin. I'm sorry, Madame. I'll stop now and we can go on with the lesson."

Mrs. Strauss had stiffened. Her fingers (magic fingers) were clenched into two small fists on the mauve fabric of her dress. She hung her head and spoke in such a low voice that Daskeh had to lean forward to hear what she was saying:

"Every day I thank God he's alive . . . every day. What matters it, not being able to play the violin when there are young men like him dead and under the earth? What matters? Even his hands he still has, and his legs—have you seen them near the hospital with no legs sometimes—and no arms. I cannot look at them. Alex is lucky. So I tell myself. . . ." Mrs. Strauss looked up. Tears were running down her cheeks and she did nothing to stop them.

She said to Daskeh, "But it *does* matter, does it not? Every single tiny thing matters—everything that is spoiled, made ugly, broken by war. And even for good causes, for good reasons, people are still hurt. In big ways and small ways. People are hurt and some get better altogether, and some get

a little bit better, but nothing stays how it was."
Mrs. Strauss shook her head and stood up.

"I go now to wash my face, child. I am glad to
have a son who is alive. I am crying for other
mothers not so fortunate. You will play B-flat mi-
nor scale with both hands. Two octaves, till I re-
turn. I will listen from the bathroom."

Daskeh's fingers found the notes. Mechanically,
she played the scale up and down the piano, again
and again without seeing the keys at all. She saw
Alex sitting in the darkened salon, and Danny
dreaming of the metal skeletons of trucks burning
on a dusty hillside.

The following week, Daskeh persuaded Danny to
go with her to the music lesson.

"It's pointless lying on your bed and moping,"
she said. "Walk with me. Look at all the shops.
It'll take your mind off . . . well, off your troubles.
And you need some air. You look awful."

That was true. Danny had purple smudges under his eyes from not sleeping, and his thin white
face was thinner and whiter than usual. Daskeh
had told him about Alex. "He's Madame's son.
He's very nice and he used to be a real soldier.

He's hurt his hands and he's staying with his mother till he's better."

"I don't want to meet him," said Danny. "What makes you think I want to see a real soldier? I'd be embarrassed, because I'm such a coward, I'm even scared of my dreams."

"Oh, for heaven's sake, Danny!" said Daskeh. "Just come to the music class. Let your life be normal at least when you're not sleeping! And I'll buy you a doughnut. You look as if you could use one, too, I can tell you. Skinny as a rake!" She smiled, and Danny agreed to go.

"Your stomachache is better, I see," said Mrs. Strauss to Danny. "I am very pleased. Come, we will go straight in to the piano, and after your lesson, I will put you in the salon to wait for Daskeh, and you will have some of my strudel . . ."

Danny opened his mouth to tell Mrs. Strauss he'd just had a doughnut, and then closed it again. He knew that when Mrs. Strauss decided her pupils should take some refreshment, they were well advised not to argue.

"Is Alex here?" said Daskeh.

"He has gone for a walk," said Mrs. Strauss. "Later, perhaps he will be here."

Danny went in to his lesson feeling relieved. He knew Daskeh would be disappointed. He couldn't imagine why she wanted him to meet this Alex so much. Whatever would he, Danny, have to say to someone who had been heroic enough to be injured in battle? He sat on the piano stool and tried to concentrate on arpeggios. Music was comforting. Music was safe.

After his lesson, Danny sat in the salon, washing bites of apple strudel down with iced lemonade and listening to Daskeh playing her Mozart. Apart from the music, which sounded ghostly and distant through the closed door, there was nothing but silence all around him. He could hear no voices from the street, no traffic noises, no radios playing in other apartments. The heat pressed down on his head like an iron, even in this room that had been darkened to keep it cool. Danny felt exhaustion pulling him down, dragging at all his limbs, weighing on his eyelids. He closed his eyes. Just for a second, he thought sleepily. I'll open them soon. Very soon. Somewhere, a door banged, and Danny's eyes flew open. He shook himself a little to make sure he was properly awake.

"Hello!" said a tall young man, coming into the room. "You must be Danny."

"Yes," said Danny. "I am. But how do you know?"

"Well, I'm Alex, Mrs. Strauss's son, and she told me that you and Daskeh were coming today. I remember Daskeh from last week. You were sick, I think. You had a stomachache, but I can see you're better because you've eaten some of my mother's strudel." The young man flung himself onto the sofa, which looked too small to hold him. He grinned at Danny. "Aren't I a good detective?"

"No," said Danny, grinning back. "I never did have a stomachache. That was just what Daskeh told your mother."

Alex sat up straight. "Aha! The mystery deepens! Why should someone *without* a stomachache pretend that he is someone *with* a stomachache? Don't tell me. Let me guess. You hadn't done enough practice on your scales and you were terrified that my mother would smack you across the fingers with a ruler!"

Danny burst out laughing. "No, no, Madame never hits us. That's not the reason. The reason is . . ." Danny hesitated. "I didn't want to say what was *really* the matter with me. It was . . . silly. Embarrassing."

"Honestly? Then let me guess again. I'm looking for embarrassing ailments. A boil on your bottom that prevented you from sitting on a piano stool? No? A bad attack of smelly feet? No? You woke up and found that your fingers had turned into pickled cucumbers? No? I give up. You'll have to tell me."

"I can't."

"But you must, otherwise curiosity will make me explode."

"You'll laugh."

"Will you tell me if I promise not to laugh?"

"All right," Danny said, and immediately thought: Why am I going to tell him? I *want* to tell him. I want to tell him everything. Why?

"I'm ready," said Alex. "Don't keep me in suspense. I promise I won't laugh, however funny it is."

~

I'll say it very quickly, Danny thought, and then it'll all be over. "I have bad dreams. I hate them so much that I try not to sleep, and then I get tired. That's all. I'm sorry."

Alex didn't laugh. He didn't even smile. He sat frozen, like a statue, looking straight in front of him, and not seeing anything. Danny didn't know what to do. What had happened? Was Alex teasing him? What should he say? Should he say anything? The silence grew and grew and filled the shadowy room. After what seemed like minutes, Alex turned to look at him.

"Danny, don't be sorry." He stood up and walked over to the window. "What you've been going through is much worse than any stomachache. I don't think it's embarrassing or silly at all. In fact, I know it isn't."

"You know?" Danny felt bewildered. Alex came back to the sofa and sat down heavily. He looked at Danny and smiled.

"I have the most terrible dreams, Danny. Do you see these hands?" He held up two bandaged hands. "I won't take the bandages off. There's nothing very pleasant under them, I can tell you that, but it's beautiful compared with what I have to look at while I sleep. I was burned, you see. And some of my friends . . . well, they would have been very pleased to have escaped with injured hands. So I try to console myself. I try to tell myself that the dreams will fade. That the memories will get paler and paler as time goes on. My doctors tell me that is what will happen. But it's bad, isn't it, while it lasts? Quite bad enough to make you miss a piano lesson. Tell me what you dream about."

"Bab-el-Waad," said Danny. "I dream I'm in a truck that's on fire and the fire is getting nearer and it's going to be all around me in a minute, so I have to wake up."

"That sounds very like my dreams," Alex said. "Except in mine, I have to go into a burning room . . . in a burning house . . . to bring somebody out, and I never know who it is I'm trying to save, becuse I can never find them. . . ." Alex's voice faded to silence.

"I thought," Danny whispered, "that I was stupid. Cowardly, to be scared of dreaming about such things. I didn't know that soldiers have bad dreams too."

Alex laughed. "Soldiers have worse dreams

than anyone else, because they see and do worse things than almost anybody else. If they didn't have dreams, they would be machines and not people."

"Daskeh's father," said Danny, "told her that if you had a nightmare and you talked about it to someone, that made it better. Do you think that's true?"

Alex said, "I feel better. Don't you? Just talking to you has made me feel more cheerful. How about you?"

"I'm relieved," Danny said. "I thought it was me. Just me. But I wish . . ."

"What? What do you wish?"

"I wish Bab-el-Waad could be cleared up. I wish they'd take all the metal skeletons and bury them. Get rid of them, so that no one needs to see them anymore and get bad dreams from thinking about them."

"No," said Alex. "It's important that people should see it. As often as they can bear to look. It's important that everyone remembers exactly what it is that war can do, and what war looks like. It might prevent them from fighting again. It might teach them to search more carefully for peace."

Danny said, "Yes. Yes, I suppose you're right." He smiled at Alex. "Do you think I could have another piece of strudel? Suddenly, I'm hungry."

"Certainly," said Alex. "Please do. And I'll have a bit as well. I'm also hungry."

They sat and munched quietly in the salon, and Daskeh's music came to them from behind the door of the next room, falling around them like a cooling mist, like a blessing.

CARDBOARD BOXES
FULL OF AMERICA.
1954.

*W*henever Malka looked out the dining-room window, she was hoping for
a glimpse of Aviva, the daughter of Dr. and Mrs.
Masner, who lived across the street. Sometimes,
at night, the Masners forgot to draw their curtains, and the full glory of the lighted room beyond the glass could be seen as clearly as if it were
a stage in a theater, brightly lit and waiting for the
actors. The furniture was modern—so modern

that Malka felt she recognized it from some shop window or other. The wood was pale and yellowish, and the upholstery was striped. The walls were full of pictures that were also modern: ladies with eyes and noses in strange places, and paintings of houses with animals floating in the sky above them. There was a lace mat on the dining-room table with a cut-glass vase on it. The Sabbath candlesticks (which Malka only ever saw on Friday evenings when they were on the table) were made of silver, elaborately decorated. The Masners were rich, that was clear, and they not only *were* rich, they looked it. Dr. Masner was a dentist and wore dark suits and very shiny shoes. Mrs. Masner had a permanent wave put into her hair every few weeks by Shulamit, the chief hairdresser at Chez Yolande on Allenby Road. This Malka knew because Shulamit was one of her mother's friends. She (Mrs. Masner) wore dresses all the time, and Malka had never seen her in an apron. Perhaps she wore one in the kitchen and was careful to take it off before she came into the dining room, or perhaps (Malka liked this version the best) the Masners had a servant who spent her days slaving away over a hot stove, or working her fingers to the bone, and who was allowed into the grander rooms only in order to clean and polish and dust.

Even the Masner apartment, however, was not splendid enough for Aviva Masner. Malka had never seen a real princess, but she was sure that Aviva looked like one. She had two long, blond braids hanging down her back, and these braids were always smooth and shiny, and never had any straggling hairs escaping from them. Her brow was wide and pale, in spite of playing in the sun, and her eyes were blue. Malka had blue eyes too, but they were washed-out-looking and sometimes greenish, and her eyelashes and eyebrows were red, just like her wild, curling hair. Aviva's eyes were like a summer sky and her eyelashes were thick and quite dark. She was beautiful. Everybody in Malka's apartment block and in Aviva's own building wanted to be her friend. When the girls gathered in the yard behind Malka's building to play, there was fierce competition to be Aviva's partner, to lend her a jump rope, to be chosen for her team. Dafna, Maya, Hannah and especially Nurit were Malka's best friends, but she hadn't seen very much of them lately. She had been too busy trying to get into Aviva's gang.

"Why don't you walk to school with Nurit any-more?" Malka's mother asked.

"She goes too early," Malka answered. "I'd rather wait and go later."

The truth was that if she went later, she could time it carefully and bump into Aviva as she came out of her building, and if Irit, Liora and Ronit weren't with her, then she, Malka, would be al-lowed to walk along beside her all the way to school. It was true that Aviva never spoke in a very interesting way. She wasn't nearly as much fun as Nurit. In fact, she had a habit of not listen-ing properly, and of looking not at you but at a spot two meters above your head, as if there were someone more important standing just behind you. Malka forgave her, though, because she had such perfectly ironed blouses and such extremely white ankle socks and her sandals—every day!—looked as if they'd come out of the box from the shoe shop that very second. Nurit was always waiting for Malka at school, by the gate.

"I don't know how you can bear to walk with that Aviva," she said. "She's boring and stuck-up."

"She's not boring," Malka said. "It's just that I don't know her well enough. She's quite shy. I'm sure she's fascinating when you get to know her. Everyone wants to be friends with her, to be one of her gang. I'm not the only one."

"I don't want to," said Nurit. "So there. Anyway, you've been walking to school with her for ages, and you've been sucking up to her in the playground, and it still hasn't worked, has it? You're still not in her gang, are you?"

"I do not suck up to her!"

"You do."

"I do not."

"Oh, come on, let's go in now. I'm sick of talking about Aviva."

Malka followed Nurit into the classroom. Aviva sat far away from them, next to the window. At home, she was forced to play with children from nearby buildings who all used the same yard, but at school she went about with the girls who lived in big houses in Rehavia and pretended she hardly knew her own neighbors, apart from Irit, Liora and Ronit, of course, who were, thought Malka, like Aviva's ladies-in-waiting.

~

One morning, toward the end of the long summer vacation, a small yellow card arrived in the mail.

"Look, Malka!" said her mother. "There's another package waiting for us at the post office. A package from America!"

Malka said, "When can we go and get it? Can we go today? Can we go now? Or this afternoon? I can't bear to wait for it, not even for a second."

"We'll go this afternoon," said Malka's mother, trying to sound grown-up and organized. Malka knew that her mother was almost as excited as she was herself. There was nothing in the world as wonderful as a package from America. Since she was a baby, Malka had thought of America as a Paradise full of beautiful things, like the oil-cloth on the dining-room table, the tall tea glasses with red and blue flowers painted on them, and the shiny white handbag with a clasp that looked like a gold butterfly. Whenever anyone asked, "Where did you get such a treasure?" the answer would always come flying back: "From our relatives in America!"

When she was small, Malka imagined the whole of America to be a huge shop, a kind of department store, and she pictured her aunts walking along between the counters, choosing delightful items to put in cardboard boxes. As she grew older and began to go to the Zion Cinema with Nurit and Maya on Friday afternoons before the arrival of the Sabbath, she saw other pictures of America. It was a big country, she knew from her geography lessons, and she could see that it needed to be if it was to contain ranches with cowboys and lots of cows and horses in them, and little dusty Western towns and mountains (also full of cowboys) and cities crowded with tall gray buildings called skyscrapers, full of men in suits and ties and ladies in high-heeled shoes and dresses with skirts that stuck out and round white collars. There were also movies in which an actress called Esther Williams did a lot of swimming, and those had tropical beaches in them, and some films were about long ago and had ladies in crinolines swishing all over the place, but they all filled the screen with bright colors and music and movement, and they packed Malka's head with glorious pictures. Now she imagined her aunts and uncles worked in offices and lived in homes like those favored by Doris Day, and she and Nurit used to cut out photographs of movie stars from every newspaper and magazine they could find and glue them into big scrapbooks.

Malka thought about her scrapbooks while she waited for the morning to pass, waited for the time to come when the parcel could be collected. Earlier, Nurit had called to see if Malka wanted to go to the zoo.

"I'm going with my mother to fetch a parcel from the post office. And besides, we've seen the animals hundreds of times."

"I don't care," Nurit answered. "I like them. I like them better than I like some people. But another package from America! You are lucky. I wish we could get one."

At last, the clock crept around to the afternoon, and it was time to start.

"We'll take the bus," said Malka's mother, "because otherwise the sun will flatten us both. And of course we'll have to take a bus back, because the package will be too heavy to carry through the streets."

Malka hated buses. As soon as the doors opened, everyone who was waiting pushed to get on. There was always someone carrying something bulky or difficult. Once, it was an old woman holding five live chickens by their yellow legs as if they were a bunch of squawking flowers. Today, Malka thought, on the way back it'll be us, trying to hold the package on our laps, if we're lucky enough to get a seat. Often you had to stand. I wish I were a grown-up, Malka thought. Then I wouldn't have to look at so many belts and vest pockets and girdled bottoms. I bet the Masners never have to ride on buses. I bet they take taxis everywhere.

"Lovely! Seats for both of us!" said Malka's mother. "We can ride like two queens in our carriage."

Malka looked out the window. There was the Zion Cinema, Café Vienna, and all the little shops she liked to look at, the ones full of jewelry and silver and copper knickknacks. There were the kiosks selling fizzy red drinks that tickled your nose, and there was the man who pushed a huge pot of boiling water along the street on a cart. He had ears of cooked corn on the cob in this pot, and you could stop him and buy some. He would plunge a long fork into the water and bring out the corn as if he were spearing a golden fish. Then

~

he presented it to you like a gift, wrapped in some of its own pale green leaves. The smell came to Malka through the window of the bus and made her feel hungry.

At the post office, they had to wait in a line, and when their turn came, Malka held her breath while the man behind the metal grille looked along a whole shelf of parcels to see which one was theirs. Perhaps it was lost, perhaps it had been given to someone else by mistake, perhaps they would have to go home without it for some reason. Malka looked at the packages and tried to guess which one it could be. She did this every time a parcel arrived, and she had never once chosen the right one. When the man (oh, at long last!) found theirs, it was always bigger, more splendid, more enticing than Malka had imagined.

"It's a miracle," said the post office man from under his bushy black moustache, "that there's any of America left to send—so many people shipping pieces of it over the sea in cardboard boxes!" He waved his hand at the mountain of brown parcels behind him. "That's all I see all day—cardboard boxes full of America!"

That evening, summoned by telephone, the female members of the family gathered to divide the spoils.

"The men pretend they aren't interested in such things," said Malka's mother, "but they're very happy to wear smart American suits and drink American coffee from cans."

Malka sat and watched as wonder after wonder emerged from the opened box: dresses in colors and patterns you dream about, blouses with embroidery down the front and buttons like pearls, cans of coffee and dish cloths and towels and gadgets like potato peelers and tea strainers, and beads made out of plastic that looked, everyone agreed, "just exactly like moonstones." There were baby shoes with little rabbits or birds on them, modern shirts for the men with checks and stripes all over them, and everything came in all sorts of sizes to fit almost the whole family. For the children, there were always little boxes of raisins and shocking-pink bubble gum stuck into the corners, and also chocolate bars in vividly colored wrappers. Distributing the contents of the parcel took ages, and Malka wished it could take even longer. Every

~

item was debated, discussed, argued over.

"Will it fit Naomi?"

"Well, if not, Rivka can try it. Or Shoshanna."

"Is this shirt too big for Chaim?"

"He had a shirt last time. It's Nathan's turn."

On and on, the talk would go, around and around above Malka's head, and she only half heard it. She was too busy looking, touching, stroking and, above all, sniffing everything that came out of the box. It smelled different. It smelled particularly American, especially the comic books that she sometimes found tucked in the folds of sheets or towels whose fluffiness had been flattened by weeks of lying in a parcel. At last, everything had been taken out and its ownership decided upon. Tea was being made in the kitchen. Malka looked into the empty box.

"Hey!" she said. "You've missed this. It's a scarf."

A few cousins looked up, and Great-Aunt Pnina said, "You can keep it, Malka, I'm sure. There wasn't such a lot for you this time. No one will mind."

And it was true. Everyone was too busy cuddling her own treasures to worry about one scarf.

Malka spread it on the table in front of her.

"You can see through it," she told Great-Aunt Pnina. "Look, it's like a kind of mist."

"It's chiffon," said Great-Aunt Pnina.

"I think it's nylon," said a knowledgeable modern cousin called Ilana.

"It's so pretty," said Malka, "whatever it is. I love it."

"Wear it in good health," said her mother, who was setting the teacups out on the table.

Malka hung the scarf on the chair near her bed that night. The background was yellowy-beige, and on it were printed big flowers with pink and red and orange petals and spiky green leaves. Tomorrow, Malka thought, I'll wear it around my neck in the yard. That will show Aviva that she's not the only one with beautiful clothes.

The next day, Nurit and Malka had just finished chalking a grid on the asphalt, ready for hopscotch, when Aviva came into the yard with Irit, Liora and Ronit. Malka looked up and smiled.

"Hello, Aviva. Would you like to play hopscotch?"

"No . . . no, we're not staying very long." She

looked at Malka with more attention than she'd ever shown before. "That's a nice scarf," she said.

"She's like a magpie," Nurit muttered under her breath. "She always has a beady eye open for treasures."

"Ssh!" said Malka to Nurit. To Aviva she said: "Thank you. It came in a parcel from America." She couldn't resist boasting a little. "We often get parcels from America. We've got lots of relatives who live there."

"Really?" Aviva looked quite impressed. "You are lucky." She paused for a moment, and then she said, "It's too hot to be outside. We're going to play in my house. 'Bye." Then she turned and walked out of the yard, followed by her friends.

"The hopscotch grid is ready," said Nurit, who had continued to mark it out while Malka talked to Aviva. Malka sighed. She and Nurit hopped about halfheartedly for a while. All Malka could think about was Aviva and her friends, probably drinking iced lemonade at this very moment, up in the cool apartment. She longed to be inside with them, one of Aviva's gang, maybe even her very best friend.

"I'm going home now," she said to Nurit. "It's

too hot to hop. Do you want to come?"

"I've got to go and get some bread for my mother. Then we're going out somewhere. Will I see you tomorrow?"

"I expect so," said Malka, and added, "Maybe," because an idea had just flashed into her mind. It was such a marvelous idea that for a few moments she couldn't quite believe she'd been so clever. Oh, it was wonderful! Aviva would never be able to resist . . . but should Malka wait until she saw Aviva in the yard, or should she go up and knock on her door? She would have to talk to Aviva, and how could she do that without nearly melting with embarrassment? She needed a way of talking without being seen. She needed something like a telephone. As soon as this notion came to her, Malka said to herself: Why not the telephone? I can look in the book and find the number. Dr. Masner is sure to be in it because he's a dentist. But what will I say? How will I put it? Will I dare to talk at all?

When she reached home, Malka looked up the Masners' number and wrote it down on a piece of paper, which she put in her pocket. She thought about telephoning all through the afternoon, and then at last, while her mother was busy in the kitchen preparing supper and making a lot of clatter with dishes and pans, Malka decided to do it. She dialed the number, and then she heard the ringing tone and imagined the phone in the Masners' apartment filling the room with its loud cries.

Then someone said, "Jerusalem 26385," and Malka said, "I'd like to speak to Aviva, please."

"This is Aviva speaking. Who's that?"

"It's Malka. From across the street."

"Oh."

"I'd like to ask you something."

"Go on, then." (She sounded impatient, Malka thought.)

"I wanted to know if you like my scarf."

"I told you I did. I think it's lovely. What a stupid thing to call about." (Malka thought: Now she seems cross.)

"I wanted to ask if you'd like it as a present."

Silence, then: "You want to give me your scarf?"

"Yes."

"Why?"

~

"No reason. I just want you to have it. Perhaps I could play with you and Irit and Liora and Ronit sometimes." (Did that sound casual enough? Malka wondered.)

"Ah, I see. If you give me your scarf, I've got to let you be in our gang. Is that it?"

Malka blushed and felt happy that at least Aviva couldn't see her. Oh, well, she thought, what have I got to lose? She said, "Yes, that's it."

A very long silence followed. Malka, straining her ears, could hear whispering. Obviously, Aviva was consulting the other members of the gang. It went on for ages. At long last, Aviva came back on the line and said, "Hello, Malka? Are you still there?"

"Yes."

"It's okay. We've decided that you can be in our gang. Bring the scarf to my apartment tomorrow at ten."

"Thank you, Aviva. Yes, I will. Good-bye." She put the telephone back on its cradle and hugged herself with sheer pleasure. She was one of Aviva's gang now, a properly invited member. From tomorrow she would be one of the ladies-in-waiting.

~

Two weeks after what Malka thought of as "The Day of the Telephone Call" she walked up to the third floor of her apartment building and knocked on the door of Nurit's apartment.

Nurit opened the door, looking puzzled for a moment when she saw Malka; then her face cleared, and she smiled.

"Hello, Malka. I haven't seen you for ages."

"I know—I'm sorry. Can I come in?"

"Okay. Come into my room. Is Aviva busy? Why aren't you playing with her? I thought you were her friend now."

"I'm your friend too," said Malka. "I've always been your friend, ever since we were babies."

"But you've stopped coming to play, so I don't know if you're my friend anymore."

"Of course I'm your friend," said Malka. "I'm sorry I haven't been coming to your house so often."

"You've been busy. Is she bored with you?"

"No," said Malka. "I'm bored with her. She's not very nice, Nurit."

"I knew that. I could see she wasn't."

"How did you know? She's so beautiful, and she

has such lovely clothes."

"That," said Nurit, "isn't enough to make her nice."

"No, but I wanted to be her friend. I wanted to be asked into her lovely apartment."

"Is it lovely?"

"I suppose it is. But you can't make even the smallest mess. If you eat a cookie, Mrs. Masner comes up behind you with a dustpan and brush, and those girls never do anything. They just play dress-up and dolls. They don't go anywhere except the yard. They never go to the zoo or the movies. They've never heard of all our movie stars."

"What sort of games do they play with their dolls?"

"Hospital, mostly. They were playing that this morning when it happened . . ." Malka's voice faded to silence.

"When what happened?" asked Nurit. Malka looked up.

"Do you remember the scarf? The one that came from the last American parcel?"

"The one you gave Aviva," said Nurit. "I remember it. It was lovely."

"I *loved* that scarf," said Malka. "I dreamed about it at night after I gave it away. Well, Aviva stopped wearing it round her neck after a couple of days, and I thought she must have hung it up with her best dresses, or folded it neatly in one of her drawers. Well, yesterday when we were playing hospital, she needed a bandage, so she rummaged around in a big basket full of bits of dustcloths and old rags, and then out came the American scarf. I recognized it even though it was crumpled and dirty. 'This'll do for a bandage,' Aviva said, and she began to wrap it around the cut knee of one of her silly dolls. Irit and Liora and Ronit laughed, and I know they were really laughing at me. I wanted to hit Aviva, but I didn't dare. I wanted to tear the scarf off the doll's knee and wash it and iron it, but it was spoiled and I didn't really like it anymore. So I just said I had to go home, and I came here. I won't play with her again. She's horrible."

Nurit nodded. "There's a lovely movie at the Zion this week. It's called *By the Light of the Silvery Moon*, and it's got Doris Day in it."

"Lovely!" said Malka, and smiled at Nurit. The

next time there was an American parcel, she decided, Nurit would get something from it. It would be a present suitable for a real best friend: a little piece of America.